Contents

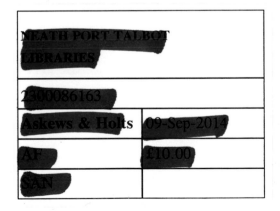

List of illustrations

About the author

LESLIE MANN was born in Singapore in 1914, the son of a police inspector. The family later moved to the UK, and Leslie started work as a sound engineer at Elstree Studios. He enlisted in the RAF in 1939, and married in 1940.

Ultimately stationed near Ripon, Yorkshire, he served as a Flight Sergeant rear gunner with No. 51 Squadron, RAF Dishforth, operating Armstrong Whitworth Whitley twin-engine bombers. He was shot down on a raid over Düsseldorf on the night of 19/20 June 1941, the only loss from twenty aircraft on that raid: all five crew were captured.

Unusually, Mann was repatriated to the UK in October 1943 and discharged from the RAF in 1944. He worked for Pathé News and later became a correspondent in the Korean War and a cameraman in Kenya during the Mau Mau uprising. He then moved to the BBC, for whom he worked as a senior news executive until retirement. He died in 1989.

RICHARD OVERY is an award-winning historian best known for his remarkable books on the Second World War and the wider disasters of the twentieth century. His most recent book, *The Bombing War*, was described by Richard J. Evans in *The Guardian* as: 'Magnificent ... must now be regarded as the standard work on the bombing war ... It is probably the most important book published on the history of the second world war this century.' He is Professor of History at the University of Exeter and lives in London.

Author's note

This story is an attempt to explain through an airman's mind his last twelve hours on a bomber station.

After the fall of France in 1940, Britain had to concentrate on fighters and defences, and Bomber Command operated as best it could, mainly for nuisance value and home propaganda. The 'leaflet raids' had stopped and bombing started in earnest. Discipline for aircrews was by no means rigid, aircraft rather outdated, and losses were high. Operations were carried out, it seemed, by trial and error, while the 'New Air Force' was being built up.

This is not a story of heroes; of men who groaned with disappointment when an 'op' was postponed or cancelled; of men who smuggled themselves out of hospital so as not to miss going with their crew on a particular raid; although, no doubt, there were men like that in the Royal Air Force.

I have tried to give a picture as I saw it.

Leslie Mann

And some fell on stony ground, where it had not much earth; and immediately it sprang up, because it had no depth of earth:

But when the sun was up, it was scorched; and because it had no root, it withered away.

Mark, 4: 5,6

Introduction

By Richard Overy

The anti-hero of Leslie Mann's fictional representation of RAF Bomber Command's offensive against Germany finds that his first thought on landing by parachute on German soil after his aircraft has been hit by anti-aircraft fire is simply 'No more ops'. This is perhaps not the popular version of the story of the heroic bomber crew who night after night ran exceptional risks over Europe, but it reflects a profound reality. For those young men who had to go 'over the top' night after night, the strain of a prolonged tour of operations was profound. This short fictional account conveys better than a hundred dry operational reports the fear and the courage that jostled side by side in the mind of almost every bomber crewman.

It is important to emphasise that this is a fictional but not a fictitious account. The details of daily life on a bomber base and the vivid description of a bomber operation were the product of a lived experience. Leslie Mann flew as a tail gunner in Whitley medium bombers and was shot down over Germany in June 1941, just like his fictional Pilot Officer Mason. He joined the Royal Air

1

Force in 1939, when it was still in the slow process of converting to more modern aircraft types. He ended up in Bomber Command, formed in 1936 when the RAF was restructured on functional lines, separating fighters, bombers and coastal defence aircraft. No one knew when the war broke out on 3 September 1939 what bomber crew would be expected to do. Bombing operations were confined to occasional forays against the German fleet; bomber crew found themselves flying over hostile territory dropping propaganda leaflets. Bombing enemy home front targets was prohibited.

All this changed in May 1940. As the German invasion of France and the Low Countries got under way from 10 May, the new Prime Minister, Winston Churchill, discussed with his cabinet the prospect of bombing German industrial and communications targets to try to slow up the German advance and to divert the German Air Force to home defence. On the night of 11/12 May, 37 bombers attacked rail and road targets in the town of Mönchengladbach. The operation included eighteen Whitleys, one of which was shot down.[1] On 15 May, the War Cabinet finally approved attacks on industrial targets from which civilian casualties might result and from that point on, long before the onset of the German Blitz in September 1940, RAF bombers undertook regular raids against targets they could reach in the industrial zones of northern and western Germany.[2] Despite optimistic expectations of both the material damage and the morale effect, the bombing achieved very little. German observers were puzzled about the purpose of it, since the attacks were wildly inaccurate, many of the bombs falling in the open countryside. At night with no electronic navigation aids, and a comprehensive blackout to combat, it proved very difficult to find even the city where the targets lay. The German air defence concluded that the British pilots had been instructed to drop their bombs to cause maximum damage to civilians and civilian housing.

The RAF continued to bomb German targets all through the Blitz period with an increasing weight of bombs, but the operational difficulties undermined the efforts made by bomber crews to try to find and hit the targets they were ordered to bomb. In October 1940 they were instructed to hit anything that looked militarily useful if they could not find their primary target. Slowly the RAF commanders realised that with the existing technology and tactics there was no prospect of inflicting anything like decisive damage on German industry. By July 1941, shortly after Leslie Mann was shot down, the decision had been made to focus attacks on the morale of the German workforce by bombing industrial city areas. This decision was taken long before Air Marshal Arthur Harris took over the Command in February 1942, though he is still widely, and wrongly, regarded as its instigator. A few weeks later in August 1941 Churchill's chief scientific adviser, Frederick Lindemann (later Lord Cherwell), published a report produced by one of the statisticians on his staff, David Butt, which showed that over the Ruhr-Rhineland industrial region only one aircraft in ten got within five miles of the designated target. Leslie Mann would certainly have understood that this was the reality of the many missions he had flown. In a note at the start of his manuscript he observes that the operations he and his fellow crewmen undertook had only 'nuisance value'.

It is not easy to understand why RAF Bomber Command persisted so long with operations that clearly had little strategic impact and cost a high percentage of the highly-trained airmen sent on each mission. Nor is it easy to explain why it took so long to produce effective navigation aids, a better bombsight and tactics that might maximise the chances of finding and hitting at least the target area. The slow development of all these operational necessities occurred long after Leslie Mann had been shot down. His account of a bombing operation comes, unusually, from the start of the campaign when its achievements and purpose were dubious, and the cost in manpower from enemy action or, very commonly, from accidents, prodigious. He was fortunate to survive, but thousands of others died in operations which the RAF commanders knew were having little effect.

The offensive made sense at this stage principally as a political instrument. Mann himself recognised that 'home propaganda' was one of the reasons why he and others were sent night after night on long dangerous flights. The raids were widely reported in the press to give the British public the news that German cities were suffering like British cities during the Blitz.[3] This was the most visible way British forces could show that the fight against Germany (and Italy) had not been abandoned. Occupied Europe, it was believed, might be encouraged to resist the occupier if the captive peoples could be confident that Britain was serious about the fight. Alongside the bombs, RAF planes dropped millions of leaflets spelling out to the French or Dutch or Belgians who read them that bombing was a step nearer to liberation.[4] The message was also directed at the American public, since it was important to demonstrate that the war was still being fought if there were to be any prospect of winning American material support for the British Empire's war effort, or of persuading President Franklin Roosevelt to intervene actively on the British side.

It might well be argued that the death of thousands of young airmen was a high price to pay for these political dividends, even though losses were much lower than the cost in lives endured in the first year of fighting in the First World War. Mann's fictional pilot reflects at one point on whether 'defeat [was] more bitter than death' or 'death sweeter than defeat', but he at once pushes the thoughts away. It was difficult to keep morbidity at bay in a world where the death of friends and companions was an everyday occurrence and the prospect of your own death a very real one every time you climbed into the cockpit or the gun turret. One of the things evident from this account is the variety of ways in which airmen reacted to the reality they faced, like so many prisoners on death row not knowing the order in which they are to be executed.

The core of Mann's account is a day and night in
the life of a bomber pilot who has been through many
missions already, seen his companions perish, and strug-
gles with his fears and thoughts each time he has to
embark on a fresh operation. On this mission, a flight
to the German Rhineland city of Düsseldorf, the fictional Mason is in a particularly reflective mood. The
mission was, in fact, a real one. The Air Ministry saw the
Ruhr-Rhineland area as the 'civil garrison of Germany's
economic citadel', which was one way of pretending that
civilian targets were, in effect, military in character.[5] On
the night of 19/20 June 1941 twenty Whitleys were
sent off on the operation and one was, indeed, lost. The
same night a larger group of Wellington bombers raided
Cologne with little success. The Cologne authorities
reported only 60 incendiary bombs and no casualties.
The rest of the bombs, like those jettisoned from Mason's
aircraft as it is hit by anti-aircraft fire, fell somewhere
other than the target.

The force of which Mann was a part in June 1941
was very small by the standards of the German Air Force
that raided Britain during the Blitz or by the standards
of the large Allied force of heavy bombers available
much later in the war. In June 1941 Bomber Command
had a total of 533 serviceable light, medium and heavy
bombers for which there were only 410 full crews available.[6] Most of them were twin-engine medium bombers,
the majority Vickers Wellingtons. By this stage of the
war there were only six operational squadrons of the

Armstrong-Whitworth Whitley bombers left; these units in July 1941 had exactly 59 serviceable aircraft and 67 full crews.[7] Mann had been a member of a tiny cohort still flying aircraft that were by now obsolescent. The whole of the bomber force undertook 3,935 sorties in June 1941, losing 99 bombers that month, of which Mann's was one. They dropped only 3,473 tons of bombs on German targets during June, a sum that could be carried in just one raid by the end of the war. It was the peak of the bombing effort against Germany in 1941, however. By September only 2,000 tons were dropped, by December only 799.[8]

The details of the operation undertaken by the fictional Mason in Leslie Mann's account paint a familiar picture, common to many descriptions of bombing raids by those who took part in them. What is different about Mann's account is the time spent analysing the long period of waiting beforehand and the thoughts and anxieties that plague the pilot as he braces himself for combat. The circumstances that bomber crews faced were very different from an army unit or a ship at sea. The most striking contrast is the environment. RAF crew based in Britain found themselves caught between civilian and military life. Off duty they were still at home, among friends, perhaps with family nearby. Their recreation was shared with the local inhabitants who regarded them with mixed enthusiasm. They could find local girlfriends, even if the relationship was likely to be brief or pointless, like Mason's moment of flirtation with a pretty girl he sees across the dance-floor. Yet even while they relaxed, hoping perhaps that the weather would worsen, the knowledge was hard to suppress that there might be a mission that night or the following night which would be their last. Mason wanted to ask the girl for a date 'but something stopped him'. There was, he reflects, an injustice in the situation in which you were both a part of daily life and yet apart from it, yearning for normality yet aware of the very abnormal world you would inhabit in a matter of hours somewhere over Germany.

The close contact with civilian life was awkward and uncomfortable and yet at the same time unavoidable, even enticing. Yet it was juxtaposed with a combat reality that was uniquely dangerous and demanding. Within minutes of leaving the local pub or the dance-hall, crew could find themselves in the lorry carrying them out to the aircraft on their stands. Within an hour they would be at 12,000 or 15,000 feet, high above the Channel or the North Sea, cold, slightly sick, anxious. Within two or three hours they would be over German territory, avoiding the searchlights, praying that the anti-aircraft fire would be inaccurate or too low, wondering if the night fighters controlled from the ground in their particular vector would home onto them or the aircraft behind, and all the time trying to navigate accurately to a blacked-out destination covered, as Düsseldorf actually was on that night of the 19/20 June, with a thick industrial haze. If they survived the raid, they would once again be back home, able if they wished to pick up where they had left off with the civilian world they had briefly abandoned.

It is difficult to decide if this situation made the airmen more anxious rather than less. The comforting cushion of a generally rural locality was in many ways so distant from the real world of combat, death or survival that it almost invariably provoked an ambiguous relationship between the civilian hosts and their temporary guests. It could also be an isolated existence. Airmen might be posted together to a base but the cohort would not survive long together. Mason mourns the loss of his close companions, as no doubt Leslie Mann found himself doing, but the loss was compounded with the problems raised by the rapid replacement of the casualties by young men for whom the 'veterans', who might have survived fifteen or twenty sorties, now seemed remote and taciturn. The newcomers worked out their own pattern of friendship and familiarity, which in turn might last little longer than the first few operations. Mann's pilot regrets that 'There was nobody he could say "Do you remember?" to', even though these were memories of only a few weeks. The effort to create new friendships while anticipating all the time their probable sudden termination grew less the longer airmen survived. The crew relationships that did develop were kept at a curious distance by the insistence that no names were to be used on board the bomber, only functions – 'Rear Gunner', 'Navigator', 'Engineer'. Mason abandons the practice in the book but it is not difficult to understand why it was used in a context where crew turnover was remorseless.

The most revealing elements in this account deal with the everyday life of young men under the strain of combat. Some of the observations are generic, some particular to the experience of the bomber crew. Most accounts of modern battle explain the willingness to fight and to continue to fight in terms of the primary group, the small units into which fighting men are usually divided. Whether a company or a platoon, or an artillery unit or a bomber crew, the small group of men depend on each other and develop in most cases a strong sense of loyalty to their immediate circle. In air operations that sense of commitment could be extended to the crews of other aircraft in the vicinity. Reading the accounts by survivors of life in Bomber Command it is evident that little thought was given to what or who was being bombed; the aircrew had a morality that was simple – to survive if possible, to help each other if difficulties arose. For bomber crew dropping the bombs was their only purpose. The words 'bombs gone' offered immediate relief, while for those on the ground who were going to be hit or killed by them the crisis was only just beginning. At this point even thinking about the other aircraft behind or around them disappeared as a moral concern. 'It was the others,' muses Mason, 'not them, who would be killed.'

The men in this small enclosed sphere all shared one emotion: fear. This was often difficult for them to admit to others because of the stigma conventionally attached to displays of fear. Yet the accounts by surviving bomber crewmen almost universally describe fear as a primary emotion in their combat experience. Fear before an operation, based on the rational expectation that there was a limit to the luck any single crew might have; fear while in the air that the weather, technical problems, engine failure and, finally, the enemy might bring the fragile aircraft crashing to the ground miles below. Fear is ever-present in combat situations, but it is not to be confused with cowardice. Indeed the greatest courage is required to master those fears and to undertake the mission. The RAF Neuropsychiatric Centre, set up to help airmen cope with the stress of flying, recognised that regular combat in the air, day after day, was likely to produce 'anxiety and depressive states'. The psychiatrists also understood that declining confidence about flying did not imply cowardice but resulted in many cases from the effects of severe flying stress.[9]

The record of many of those who were sent to the Centre showed that flying stress was indeed severe. A number of the crew who received evaluation and treatment had already undertaken many operations without becoming a psychiatric casualty, so that cowardice was never a question. Under the constant threat of death or injury, most men were found to have a threshold beyond which it was difficult to go. It was possible to undertake the required thirty missions and survive without crossing that threshold, and the selection and training regimes were supposed to ensure that men who might crack under the strain were weeded out at an earlier stage. One patient at the Neuropsychiatric clinic had been a bus conductor in civilian life before joining the RAF, but he had been referred because of a persistent stammer and nail-chewing. The clinic concluded from their examination that the patient had a strong predisposition to psychotic behaviour and should never have been selected in the first place. Other patients were there because they had extreme experiences which would have tested the psychological robustness of the sternest personality. One pilot with 200 hours of operational flying had ditched in the North Sea, been badly shot up in a raid over Essen, had seen his navigator killed, and had finally reached his threshold. He shook uncontrollably, slept badly and confessed to wanting to cry. The psychiatrists discovered that he was an only child with a nervous mother, and once again ascribed some of his condition to a predisposition to neurotic behaviour, even though in this case the experiences alone might well have provided a sufficient explanation.[10]

What every airman wanted to avoid was the accusation of a 'Lack of Moral Fibre'. This was the category used to describe those who reacted against further flying but who neither demonstrated a predisposition to neurosis nor had been subjected to gruelling operational experiences. These few were defined as 'waverers', fully fit in mind and body but fearful of flying. About one-quarter of those sent for assessment were deemed not to be medical cases and their cases went before an executive board to decide their fate. Not all of the 8,402 RAF men (and a few women) examined for neurosis were considered

LMF cases, but over the course of the war 1,029 of them were classified this way, 37 per cent of them pilots. It has been estimated that around one-third of all the psychiatric cases referred came from Bomber Command, an average of less than twenty a month, a remarkably small figure given the stresses to which the men were subjected.[11] The few designated LMF had to go through the indignity of being stripped of their rank and sent to do some demeaning job away from the force. This was in itself a strong incentive to try to hide any physical symptoms of anxiety or for colleagues to shield the sufferer from authority. Mann's pilot is more candid. When one crewman becomes literally paralysed by fear ('moist grey face ... horribly staring eyes ... white knuckles gripping the ledge') he is reported to the commanding officer. It was generally understood that a psychiatric casualty on board was a liability for the whole crew, which was undoubtedly the case. But they could qualify for therapy and counselling and in a small number of cases were returned to flying duties, their record unimpaired.

For airmen who stayed at the job and survived, the longer it went on, the worse it got. The odds of reaching fifteen or twenty or even thirty operations were small, but the closer to the end of a tour of duty, the more desperate the urge to survive. 'The longer you lasted,' claims Mason, 'the fewer chances you could afford to take.' A pilot might certainly learn by experience and have a better chance of survival than he did on the first few trips, but accidents, poor weather or an unlucky anti-aircraft hit could end a successful run of operations any time a pilot took to the air. This anxiety was a permanent state.

Leslie Mann's pilot is certainly not immune to fear, and it must be supposed that Mann is describing his own feelings in the many passages in the book where fear raises its head. Early on in the fictional account Mason recalls his dead pilot friend 'Ken' wondering 'if my crew are as scared as I am on ops'. Mann understood that being scared and being a coward is not the same thing. At one point, as Mason contemplates a new loud-mouthed crew member he instinctively assumes is a coward at heart, he reflects on his own feelings: 'it was difficult to decide exactly what a coward was. He, Mason, was afraid of ops. Hated them … Couldn't really blame anybody for not liking ops anyway: nobody did, though some got a kick out of the tension and excitement before, and the relief afterwards.' The strength that airmen had to find was an inner strength that gave them, somehow or other, the courage to continue to do something that they knew rationally was dangerous, even suicidal. There is a powerful passage in Mann's account that sums up the psychological effort he and perhaps a majority of the force had to go through. When a novice crew member, grinning with embarrassment, asks what it is like to go on operations, Mason thinks to himself about the answer he would like to give:

What could you tell these first-trippers? That it was bloody awful, frightening, sickeningly so, and more often fatal? That each trip got worse? That each time you got back you could hardly believe it? That the ground seemed so solid and firm and friendly and you were just about to feel happy when you realised that it only meant you were alive to go again, and again, and then again, until God knows when? That if you lasted long enough you became lonely because all your friends had gone? That you got into such a state that you had to suppress all your emotions, like anger, sentimentality, soft-heartedness, even gratitude and kindness, and certainly fear, because it made your lip quiver and you wanted to cry?

In the end he says none of this, and gives the novice a laconic reassurance: 'Oh, not so bad.'

This reaction to the operations might be regarded simply as Mann's way, long after the event, of conveying his own bitterness over what he had been expected to do, reflected upon during his years in a German prisoner-of-war camp. But there is a great deal of corroborating evidence from the accounts of other bomber crew both at the time and in memoirs or oral testimony after the war. Being asked to go 'over the top' not once or twice, but night after night made exceptional demands on the men who did it. They were mostly volunteers, but nothing imparted in the training schools or gleaned from the public press presentation of the air war would have prepared them for what it was actually like. Those who commanded them to do it – in this case Air Chief Marshal Sir Richard Peirse, commander-in-chief Bomber Command – did not fly with them to find out for themselves (unlike American commanders of the Eighth Bomber Command who flew on missions and risked death each time). So little did Peirse perhaps appreciate what he was making Leslie Mann and others do, that on the night of 7/8 November 1941 he sent off a major raid, the largest yet mounted, with most of the aircraft destined to bomb Berlin. He knew the weather outlook was not good but ordered the operation regardless. Only 73 out of 169 bombers found the German capital but bombed with poor accuracy; fourteen houses were destroyed and nine people killed. The loss rate for the Berlin part of the raid was 12.4 per cent of the force. In total 37 bombers were lost that night in conditions of high winds, storms and icing – and all for negligible effect. The raid cost Peirse his job, but the Command lost over 180 men.

Of course at the time the precise results of the raids could not be known, though photo reconnaissance afterwards could betray how limited was the evidence of damage. Crews were always told that they were attacking an important industrial centre or target whose destruction would shorten the war. Crews had to think that despite all the terrors an operation provoked, it had some purpose. Mann remarks that airmen wanted to drop as many bombs as quickly as possible so that the war would be over sooner. They accepted that what they did must be achieving something because to believe the opposite would have made the operations not only fearful and demanding, but pointless as well. Mann understood that it was important for an airman if he survived to have a clear conscience and his pride intact, and that these feelings would come first and foremost from knowledge that he had done his best under trying circumstances to fulfil his duty, chiefly to himself but also to the aims of the Command. In a striking passage, Mann argues that these feelings have 'nothing to do with patriotism'. 'It is doubtful,' he continues, 'if anybody is ever willing to die for his country, or its king, its people, its mountains or its fields, its valleys or its beaches, its industries or its politicians.' At one level those fighting the war doubtless knew that there were important, if often vaguely defined war aims; but in the cauldron of combat this is not what ordinary men are likely to be thinking about. In this case getting there, dropping the bombs and surviving the trip back absorbed all their cognitive energy.

It was to be true to his conscience and his pride that Leslie Mann carried on operations despite every instinct to shy away from the risks and dangers. That conclusion comes across strongly from his account of an airman's experience, living permanently in the shadow of death. But Mann's pilot also thought that it would be good to find that operations might be suspended temporarily or even permanently for reasons beyond your control, such as injury or illness. One of the crew from the aircraft whose crash ended the life of his close companion 'Ken', was so seriously injured that he would not return to operations; 'one of the lucky ones' is how Mason describes him. The American Eighth Air Force statistics on personnel had a category for those men who had survived a tour of thirty operations and were returning to the United States headed 'Happy Warriors'.[12] The other possibility was to become a prisoner-of-war. You ran some small risk that during the war you might be killed by the bombing of your own side, and some were.[13] But in general, becoming a POW ended the nightmare of operations: 'no more ops', as Mason realises once he has landed on German soil.

The sense of relief is evident in one of the first letters Leslie Mann sent back from imprisonment to his wife Joan, expecting their first child. Only a day after his aircraft had been hit and he had parachuted safely to earth with the rest of the crew, he was able to write home: 'being very well treated. Plenty of food ... all the crew are well too.'[14] A day or so later he wrote a second letter in which his relief at the end to his ordeal is evident:

I hope by now that you have heard I am a prisoner of war. It must have worried you a bit when you heard I was missing. That was rather worrying for me. We were shot down over the Ruhr on the 20th, but all managed to bale out; and at present we are all together, and are likely to remain so. We are being treated exactly as I've always said and are having a very comfortable time. Please don't worry about me, we were very lucky in getting away with it. It could have been much worse. It was bad luck for me to miss my commission by so short a time, but I am not grumbling ...[15]

The two letters were franked on the 30 June, so that Mann's wife knew very quickly that he was safe and that the anxieties generated by the possibility of his death on every mission were now over.

Imprisonment for Mann was an ordeal of a different kind. His many letters reveal what most prisoners must have felt, that the tedium of life in camp was remorseless and unavoidable. On 6 February 1942 he wrote 'all things here are the same – dates don't mean anything'.[16] And indeed they did not: for most of January 1942 he wrote January 1941 at the top of his letters. Mann tried to learn German. He had a spell in hospital which he treated the way he might have done on operations, as a lucky relief from the routine of prison camp life in Stalag [Stammlager] IX-C. Mann was not unusual in his longing to be back home again and his letters throughout 1942 and 1943 return again and again to the same themes. On a card on 24 April 1942 he scribbled at the foot: 'P.S. Wanna get home.'[17] It was difficult to maintain the mask of artificial good humour which the limited space and the role of the censor encouraged. In May 1943 he admitted that 'in our "dark moments", which we all get, our whole outlook gets sort of clouded over'. A few months later, in a more candid letter about the 'beastly existence' in the camp he explains that some airmen, despairing of the endless imprisonment, regretted parachuting to safety: 'I've actually heard blokes say they wished they'd stayed in their machines, and meant it …'[18] He hastened to reassure his wife that he had never said that, and never would, and everything about his attitude to operations expressed in his manuscript makes that clear. He, too, was one of the lucky ones, even if he had to endure years of maddening incarceration.

Just as the airmen in the book speculate all the time about how soon the war will be over, so the prisoners-of-war hoped month after month that the war would be terminated quickly (and victoriously) so that they could return to normal life. In the late months of 1941 Mann was optimistic that the war would soon be over and he would be reunited with his family. In the spring of 1942 he bets with the camp medical officer about when the war will end in the hope, perhaps, that it will somehow make eventual release seem more real. But by 1943 there is evidence of a growing pessimism. Prisoners got little news of what was actually going on in the world outside and their German captors had no interest in telling them. The closest most of them got to the war was the noise of Bomber Command heavy bombers, which they had not flown, droning through the darkness on another operation, and from 1943 onwards the occasional sight of Eighth Air Force B-17s and B-24s gleaming in the sky high above them on daylight raids. As it turned out, Leslie Mann was lucky a second time. Deemed to be a psychiatric casualty, he was repatriated by the International Red Cross in the autumn of 1943. He did not return to Bomber Command but instead found a job with Pathé News. His fictional account of his year in Bomber Command was written, as far as we know, in the late 1940s.

And Some Fell on Stony Ground is an ironic title, symbolising perhaps Mann's own sense of the futility of what he and fellow crewmen in Bomber Command were being asked to do. As an account of the psychological demands of combat in exceptional circumstances it has about it a striking honesty. This is not quite the image of the bomber force manufactured by the media and much popular history, which is bland and heroic, where this account is bitter and self-effacing. The value of Leslie Mann's perspective lies in the explanation it gives of how it was possible for young men to endure this degree of combat stress and to continue flying. This is a question likely to be prompted by any study of the long bombing campaign. With the passage of time, this is a question that might be asked about the millions of men (and a large number of women) plucked from civilian life who found themselves faced with the gruelling prospect of combat in the air, at sea, on the many ground fronts and in the wartime resistance. For Leslie Mann and his generation, fighting a war did not seem as strange a demand as it would now seem in Western countries seventy years later. The experience of bombing, like the earlier experience of the trenches, is now history. As the anniversaries of these wartime experiences pile up, accounts such as this are a ready reminder of just how fortunate Europeans have been to live through three-quarters of a century of relative peace.

Richard Overy

2. Armourers wheel trolleys of 500-pound bombs towards the open bomb bay of an Armstrong Whitworth Whitley of No. 58 Squadron RAF at Linton-on-Ouse, Yorkshire. Leslie Mann flew in Whitleys with No. 51 Squadron at RAF Dishforth, a few miles from Linton-on-Ouse.

3. Mechanics overhauling the Rolls-Royce Merlin X engines of a Whitley Mark V of No. 102 Squadron at Driffield, Yorkshire.

4. *(above)* An aircrew of No. 58 Squadron load parachutes on board their Whitley in preparation for a sortie, June 1940.

5. *(right)* A sergeant at the controls of a Whitley, showing the cramped conditions in which the pilot and his co-pilot had to operate.

6. *(top)* Armourers install .303-inch Browning machine guns in the rear turret of a Whitley of No. 58 Squadron after routine maintenance, June 1940.

7. *(bottom)* Interior of the rear gun turret of a Whitley, showing the trigger buttons and breech blocks of the Browning machine guns, loaded with belts of ammunition. It was in this confined space that Leslie Mann flew his missions as a rear gunner.

8. *(left)* The crew of a Whitley of No. 102 Squadron study their route before a leaflet-dropping sortie over Germany.

9. *(below)* A battery of German 88mm anti-aircraft guns opens fire, circa 1940. These fearsome weapons created most of the 'flak' that Allied bomber crews faced on their missions.

10. *(above)* Aircrew of No. 58 Squadron undergo a briefing by the Station Commander in the Operations Room, prior to an operation.

11. *(left)* Following a final briefing, men of No. 35 Squadron check their equipment before setting off on a sortie, Linton-on-Ouse, Yorkshire.

12. A Whitley of No. 10 Squadron RAF based at Leeming, Yorkshire, in flight. This aircraft went missing while on a raid over Düsseldorf on 28 December 1941.

13. A Cecil Beaton photograph of an RAF bomber crew being debriefed by the squadron Intelligence Officer on their return from a night raid over Germany, 1941.

14. A Whitley of No. 58 Squadron takes off on a night sortie.

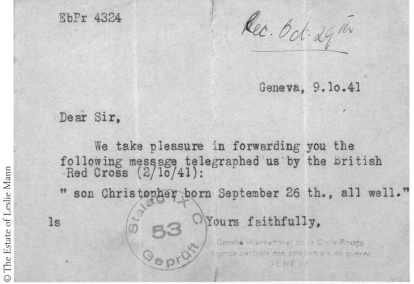

EbPr 4324

Rec. Oct. 29th

Geneva, 9.1o.41

Dear Sir,

We take pleasure in forwarding you the
following message telegraphed us by the British
Red Cross (2/1o/41):

" son Christopher born September 26 th., all well."

ls   Yours faithfully,

Comité International de la Croix-Rouge
Agence centrale des prisonniers de guerre
GENÈVE

Stalag IX C
53
Geprüft

15. Telegram sent to Leslie Mann in October 1941 while a prisoner of war
at Stalag IX-C, informing him of the birth of his son Christopher.

AND SOME FELL
ON STONY GROUND

1

One hot sunny evening in June 1941, an airman walked
slowly, rather heavily perhaps, into the pretty little village of Tackworth, turned the corner and made for the
Falcon Inn.

The door was open and at the bar he ordered a beer.
He asked if they had any cigarettes. The woman serving,
whose smile had faded from her face as she left a group
of dart-playing locals to serve him, shook her head, said
'No, sorry' and walked away. She rejoined the group, who
had been quietly watching while she served him, and
immediately began smiling and chatting again.

The airman's gaze followed her as he began to drink.
He was thinking what a stupid, ugly, ill-mannered bitch
she was.

He finished his drink quickly and walked out into
the sunshine. After standing outside for a moment, he
turned and started in the direction from which he had
come. There was no other pub between Tackworth and
the nearest town, six miles away. Might as well go back
to camp. He hated the idea of spending the rest of the
evening without cigarettes. It seemed to worry rather
than anger him.

As he approached the half-house half-shop which

also served as a post office, he thought it must be still open, because a man emerged and disappeared into a cottage next door. His hand had been clenched as though holding something.

The airman entered the shop, and asked the woman in there if she had any cigarettes.

He could see she was about to give the usual answer, but instead looked him in the face, down to his pilot's wings and back to his face. With a kindly smile she said quietly, 'I think so'.

The airman's eyes expressed his thanks far more than his answering half-smile.

It seemed strange that neither of them spoke while she was reaching below somewhere for the cigarettes and he was feeling for his money. There was plenty to talk about – the brilliant cloudless weather had been going on for weeks and the cigarette shortage much longer.

'Here you are', she said, and handed him a large packet.

'Thank you', he said, 'very much.'

He slipped the packet into his pocket and walked out of the shop.

She watched him go, still with that kindly, rather sad look. The sun was still very hot although it was seven o'clock.

He took out a cigarette, lit it, and began his walk back to camp, half a mile out of the village, glancing back at the shop as he went. The woman was still watching him, so he turned away.

As he walked he looked up at the sky, a habit of his these days. The sky was all-important to him now – in his mind always. It was so huge, so endless. It both frightened and fascinated him. The sky could kill him whenever it wanted to. It could become angry and destroy his aircraft in its wrath. It could deceive him into taking off, then make it impossible for him to land. It could peacefully and blandly lead him into Germany to be shot down by fighters or flak. It could even play cruel tricks like getting him lost by forming cloud barriers which looked like a certain coastline, even a particular point of a coastline. On those occasions it would sit back and watch his anxious and frightened efforts to find somewhere to land before his petrol ran out. And then again, with playful treachery, it would suddenly, perhaps deep inside enemy territory, on a black night, make small clouds, or a star or two, appear to be attacking the aircraft. Sometimes, even going so far as to make them appear to be crashing blindly into him, causing him instinctively to crouch with both arms guarding his face and head, a sickening feeling in his stomach – his mind a whirl of pictures of burning wreckage, dancing couples, crushed sizzling bodies, the local bus at home, a girl's face, beer and blood.

He wondered what it was going to do tonight. What trick it had in store for him.

'Bloody awful day. Not a cloud anywhere.' The current RAF expression ran through his mind.

In about three hours' time he would be up there, flying twice round the circuit to gain height – that meant

twice over that old bitch in the pub and twice over
the kind lady in the post office. Then off to Germany.
He turned his head in the direction he would take. He
knew it so well now: Flamborough Head, last pin-point
in England, then the long North Sea crossing, until, with
pulse quickening, the enemy coastline. Then, in tonight's
case, Düsseldorf, in the Ruhr valley.

'If this is my last trip', he was thinking, 'I hope that
lady in the post office hears about it.'

This thought of the last trip had now become part of
him. He couldn't, of course, remember exactly when he
had first begun to think of it, but he remembered how
he and Ken used to discuss it. It seemed years ago. He
wondered if Ken's face was still shrivelled and charred
like it was the last time he saw it – the day after the crash,
the day before he died.

As usual, thinking of Ken, he asked himself once more
if he could possibly, in some mysterious way, have been
the cause of Ken's death. And Freddie Millet's. Nonsense,
of course, all this supernatural business, superstitions and
so on. Funny, though, that Freddie had been killed the
night after they'd had curry together in that little restau-
rant in the town. And then the same with Ken. Neither of
them had really liked curry, but on those two occasions
he had managed to get his own way.

He was getting ridiculous now. All the same he
hadn't had curry since. At Ken's funeral in the village
cemetery, he kept thinking about it, telling himself
he'd have curry that night because he felt like it. Then

he felt guilty because he wasn't paying attention to the service.

It was a dreadful funeral anyway, the party made up as it was of half-trained, embarrassed, semi-interested airmen, the ragged volley made worse by one rifle jamming and going off several seconds late.

That evening he and Bill Bailey got drunk. Bill had a fight with a soldier who accused him of having loafed about in English pubs while he, the soldier, was being bombed on Dunkirk beach. An RAF policeman interfered and was immediately attacked by the soldier. Nobody got hurt but Bill and himself were brought before the C.O. in the morning. 'Sergeant Bailey and Sergeant Mason', the C.O. said, trying to look stern because the Station Warrant Officer was also in the room, 'consider this a reprimand. All right.' He nodded dismissal and, as the Warrant Officer turned smartly to march them out, gave a wink that used every muscle on one side of his face. The C.O. knew it was nobody's fault really. Ken's, if anybody's.

Poor frightened Ken, laughing about his fear. 'You know', he had once said, quietly, so that nobody else could hear, pulling on a flying boot, 'I often wonder if my crew are as scared as I am on ops.' He had said that more or less seriously but suddenly burst into laughter. 'Christ, if they only knew.'

The sky had killed Ken, by making itself pitch black, knowing that he would be tired, mentally exhausted, and a little careless at judging distances through the relief of getting home safely, so far. The irony of it was that although it had been a very nasty trip, everyone had got back. An arms factory in Czechoslovakia, difficult to find and heavily defended, and Ken had been first home, having found the target more quickly than the others and started a fire for the others to bomb.

It was Wood, sitting in the navigator's seat of Mason's aircraft, who first noticed that something was wrong down there on the airfield when they got back that cold January morning. The first suggestion of dawn was visible as they flew in over the aerodrome. There was a glint of frost on the ground.

'Something's going on down below', Wood said, standing up to get a better look. 'Lot of lights moving about.' He peered. 'And I think I can see smoke.'

There did seem to be a bit of confusion down there. 'A sneak raider, perhaps', Mason told Wood, 'waiting for us all to get back. Couldn't stay any longer because it's getting light. Watch out for him, tail gunner.'

'Right.'

They got the green light in the normal way and on landing taxied to the dispersal point.

'What's up?' he heard Wood, first out, ask a mechanic.

'"A for Apple". Written off.'

'A for Apple'? That was Ken. Mason sat there in the cockpit and let the others go past him. Written off? Perhaps it wasn't as bad as it sounded – they might have got out. Everything in the aircraft had gone quiet, except for odd clicking sounds as stresses relaxed. He and Ken were the last of the old crowd.

'Everything all right, skipper?' asked the mechanic as Mason climbed down. It was cold and gloomy on the ground.

'Yes, thanks. Fine. Flew like a bird.' He could hardly see the chap in the darkness. 'Did they get out of "A for Apple"?'

'Two did, then the main tanks ...'

'Which two?'

'Don't know, Sergeant, I just heard that two had got out.'

'Any idea what happened?'

'I think he overshot and opened up to go round again, and stalled.'

The rest of the crew had crowded round the mechanic but he couldn't tell them any more except that the two survivors had been taken off in the ambulance.

In the tender on the way to the crew-room nothing was said about the crash. They passed quite close to the still smouldering heap and in the darkness could just make out the figures of the fire squad moving about around the wreckage. Here and there bits were still glowing and as they watched a piece suddenly flared up, burnt brightly, wavered, then sank, like the triumphant leer of a witch, who, having wrought her havoc, was content to die.

On the way to the Ops Room after they had discarded their flying kit, Drake, the tail gunner, caught up and walked alongside.

'Whose machine was that?' he asked, as though he really wanted to know and was not asking out of morbid curiosity.

'Ken Minty's.'

Drake was silent for a moment or two before he said, in the same quiet way, 'His wireless op's a friend of mine. We trained together.' That was all. They walked on in silence. In the Ops Room nothing out of the ordinary had happened. The routine of taking down notes about the trip, aircrews' statements, checking the track of each aircraft on the huge map on the wall, was being done as it always was, with casual efficiency. Nobody was wearing a respect-for-the-dead look. The C.O. was there, in pyjamas and greatcoat. He was sitting on the corner of the table where the statements were being taken, swinging a leg. He smiled in his pleasant way as they approached.

'Morning, Mason', he said, including the others. 'All right?'

'Yes, sir. No trouble.' Couldn't ask about the crash yet – wasn't done. As far as this room was concerned it was all part of the night's operations. Had to drop it in casually, just to fill a gap in the conversation. The chance came when he was talking to the Plotting Officer.

'Well', the officer said, putting down the ruler he had been using on the map, and sitting on the desk. 'You're the last. Quite a successful trip. Everybody's claimed at least one hit in the target area.'

He followed the officer's gaze to the map, and staring at it said, as casually as he could, 'I've just heard about "A for Apple". Who were the two who got out, do you know?'

'Yes, Minty and Saville. God knows how they got out. They were found staggering around the wreckage.'

'They're in sick quarters, I suppose?'

'No, I heard the Doc say … that reminds me, I wanted to see him before he went back.' His eyes wandered round the room. 'He was here a moment ago.' Then louder, 'Has anybody seen the Doc?' Nobody had, apparently. Turning back he continued chattily, 'New intake coming in today. He'll have to vet them.'

'What were you saying about Minty and Saville?'

'Ah yes, they're in a bad way, the Doc said. He's had them taken straight to hospital.' He peered into his coffee cup before yelling across the room, 'Any more coffee over there? Have a cup?'

'No thank you, sir, I'm off to bed.'

Dawn was breaking cold and bleak as they walked across to their billets. Drake was a little way ahead and Mason caught him up. Drake turned as he approached but didn't say anything, his face expressionless except for the look of enquiry in his eyes.

'Sorry, Drake.' There was an awkward pause. 'It was Minty and Saville who got out.'

Drake looked straight ahead. He was very tired. 'I'll write to his mother', he said. 'I spent a leave there once.'

II

The lane swung left and there on the right lay the aerodrome. The aircraft were being prepared for the trip tonight. Ground crews were bombing up, pumping in petrol, checking oil, the controls, the lights, the guns, the radio, in fact going through the whole routine as laid down by authorities who, of course, wanted the aircraft to return. They wanted them to return because they had to go again, and again, and then again. When an aircraft didn't return another one would be sent to take its place, and a new phase for that particular ground crew would begin, but the same routine.

Looking at the first aircraft that came into view, a peculiar sensation caused Mason's footsteps to falter, and he knew he had felt it before, but couldn't remember where or when. And he wanted to remember because it worried him, like forgetting an important phone number and having no record of it. It was something transmitted from the aircraft and it caused a stir in his breast. Then he remembered. A picture formed in his mind, coming slowly into focus.

It was the day on which for the first time he had turned that corner, he and the eleven others sitting in the transport, still conscious of their shining new wings

35

and the neatly packed flying kit at their feet. Up till then the journey from the station had been chattily noisy, the conversation excitedly trivial. They had finished training and were now fully qualified aircrew, going on ops. They were 'Bomber Boys'. As the transport turned the corner, the driver said, 'There she is', and everybody looked out. There was nothing new to see – they had all seen many aircraft of exactly the same type as the one which now came into sight. They had been trained to fly them. But somehow there was something different about this one. It was like coming face to face with a well known but dangerous animal, which, though fully trained, could not really be trusted. There was something sinister about it, and it seemed to be enveloped in an atmosphere of grimness and purpose, making the aircraft they had just left at the training station seem like animals of the same species, but subdued to a point of spiritless docility.

Twelve pairs of eyes travelled to each aircraft as it came into view, and watched in silence. This was it – no more fooling about, and if you suddenly decided you didn't like this sort of thing it was too late to back out. No more flippant cross-country flights, secretly comforted by the thought that if anything went wrong there was always an aerodrome or a field somewhere about to lob down on. Or, if the worst came to the worst, bale out and get a lift in a passing car. Mason remembered saying, 'We've done it now, Ken'. Ken grinned back and nodded.

The transport turned in to the main gate and stopped at the Guard Room, and while the driver went in to report, they all sat there, feeling a little foolish, like new boys on the first day of term.

A stout little Sergeant came strutting out, jumped onto a bike much too big for him, and said 'Follow me' briskly to the driver. Mason thought vaguely that somebody could have put his head into the truck and said, 'Hello, chaps', or something, but nobody did.

They pulled up at a long, brick-built, two-storey building with an entrance at one end. It was very new, the area around bearing evidence of the builders' recent and apparently hasty evacuation.

'Here yer rooms', yelled the Sergeant, as though determined to kill instantly any ideas they might have that he was a bloody hotel porter. 'Some of the rooms are occupied. Help yourselves to the others. The keys are inside, and don't lose them – when you go on ops, hand them in to the mess steward.'

They stared at him in silence from the truck as he mounted the bike and rode off, his fat backside sliding from side to side, establishing his contempt beyond all doubt.

The driver had left the engine running and that brought them to their senses. As they climbed out somebody said, 'I don't think I'm going to like that bloke'.

Bailey answered him. 'Aw, forget him. He's one of the bastards who think the war has spoilt the Air Force.'

Wright was the last man out – he usually was – and the driver moved off, rapidly, to show that the fifteen-mile-an-hour regulation did not apply to old hands like him.

Although it was only five o'clock the corridor inside the building was rather dark and the lights had not yet been fitted. The wires hung from the ceiling, knotted, without holders. There was a breathtaking smell of fresh paint and wet plaster, and the air was gritty with powdered cement. The wash-room, into which they drifted after dumping their kit, was a long room, bare except for a row of wash-basins and some shower-bath cubicles. Lying about the concrete floor were several pieces of wood which had been used to stir paint, and in one corner a bottomless, plaster-encrusted bucket lay on its side. The wash-basins and windows were splattered with dried paint and cement, and the whole place gave the impression that the builders, driven out against their will, had fought a strong rearguard action.

That evening in the mess all twelve of them kept more or less together, a sort of instinctive precaution against the slight atmosphere of hostility they found in there. There were only two or three fellows in there young enough to be aircrew, and even these seemed to pick their way warily amongst this invasion of new mess members.

Later that evening when Mason, Ken and Bill Bailey were standing at the bar and had now given up the idea of the celebration they expected to have but which somehow did not materialise, though they drank quite a lot, Bailey leant back against the bar facing the room,

both elbows on the counter, and looked around distaste-
fully. He was a little drunk and rather truculent because
it didn't make him feel elevated. Then he began to sing,
not loudly but loudly enough, and with enormous solem-
nity, 'God save our Gracious King. Long live our noble
King …'

'For Christ's sake', Ken hissed at him, looking appre-
hensively at the bewildered faces around the room.

'… God save our King.'

Ken said, 'I'm going to bed'.

'So am I', said Mason. 'Are you hanging on, Bill?'

'No', Bailey answered. 'Coming now.' He tossed back
his drink, looked around challengingly, carefully replaced
his glass, and walked unsteadily to the door.

III

All that was ... how long ago, when he had first seen the aircraft which had looked at the same time both familiar and strange? Just a year. Mason wondered how many replacements there had been at that dispersal point since that day a year ago. Whether there'd be another one after tonight.

Sometimes when an aircraft was lost, especially the first night, he would think what a shocking waste it was. He often wondered if the factory workers ever said to themselves, 'That'll do – it won't last long anyway'. No new aircraft he had ever seen had given that impression, in fact he was always amazed at the thoroughness with which even the smallest detail had been finished off. It was difficult to understand because he felt that if he were working in an aircraft factory, he would see the futility in turning out a job as though a customer was going to examine it before buying it. Couldn't imagine anyone saying, 'I'll think it over and let you know', and put off buying the thing in case he found a better one.

The life expectancy of an aircraft was very short, but no time or trouble seemed to be spared to set the dials at the exact angle, or finish off the paintwork to the last niche and corner. The knobs on the switches and levers were always of the best quality, when it wouldn't matter, if one were in a hurry, if there were no knobs at all. The things could be worked just the same.

Another thing too – there was that little aluminium ladder clamped inside the fuselage of every aircraft for the convenience of those who wanted to get in by the rear door. Mason seldom saw anybody use it – he never did. It was much quicker and far less bother to put one knee on the step and haul yourself up.

It gave him a comfortable feeling, though, to think that there were people who didn't consider it a waste, at least pretending that each aircraft made would last a normal lifetime. Perhaps that was the idea – to give the crews that comfortable feeling. Now he came to think of it, that thought gave him more comfort than anything else on his first trip. It hadn't seemed possible that all the work and money that had gone into the making of the aircraft could be wasted the first time out. And yet when the flak started coming up, that argument seemed so futile. Time and money had nothing to do with it.

There had been plenty of flak that night too. At briefing they had been told there would be.

'Mostly light stuff, though', the Briefing Officer had said, 'so if you keep above it you should be all right.'

It was a pitch black night and the sky was crowded with stars. No moon. Over Southend on the way out a couple of searchlights wavered about ineffectively. Whether they were serious or not was hard to tell, but no action was needed to avoid them.

The whole crew were doing their first op – Wood, the navigator; Plover, second pilot and bomb aimer; Long, the wireless operator; and Drake, the tail gunner. None of them were left now. They all got split up after a time and one by one their faces disappeared from the crew-room.

The journey out on that first trip dragged like hell, and nobody spoke, the drone of the engines and the darkness enclosing each one of them in a little world of his own. Alone with his thoughts and that funny feeling in his stomach.

Wood was the first to speak. 'Target coming up in ten minutes', he said, putting aside his navigator's pad. From then on the atmosphere changed, in a subtle sort of way. Wood was sitting up a little straighter than he had been, and behind him Long flashed a torch on the radio panel, causing a faint reflective glow in the cabin. The pulse of the aircraft seemed to have quickened, and the readings on the instrument panel took on a different meaning – a new significance. The mainplane stretching out into the darkness on the left looked such an easy target, and there were two of them, both vital to the safety of the aeroplane. The fierce blue-white flames coming from the exhausts couldn't be missed by a fighter behind them, surely? Below was black silence. They were still over the sea, just coming up to the coast.

'Coast coming up.' Plover's voice from the front turret brought Wood to his feet, crouching at the side window. 'The town should be over on the right', he said.

'Can't see anything yet, though.' He sat down again, still looking out.

The next few minutes went quickly. Mason expected flak crossing the coast, but nothing happened. Five thousand feet – that should be all right. There was the town, just up the coast.

Plover's voice said, 'Bombs ready'.

'Right.'

Skirting the town on the land side, Mason could see odd little lights flickering down there, necessary lights which could not be doused altogether: train signals, travelling vehicles, and dock working lights. Well inland, he swung the aircraft hard over and headed for the town.

'Over to the left a bit', Plover said. 'I can see the river. A bit more. That's it, hold her there.'

They were over the edge of the town, flying straight and level towards the harbour.

'Still left a bit more. I can see the docks now.' Plover was thankful to be doing something at last.

Suddenly, what appeared to be a firework display began. A cluster of lights, starting from one source, travelled skywards, spraying out at the top before curving over gracefully and disappearing. Then more clusters started up, suddenly appearing from unexpected places in the darkness below, until a pattern took shape and it could be seen that a curtain was encircling the harbour. One or two sprays were coming from the harbour itself. Flak ships. Flak – the word brought with it the realisation

44

that this was gunfire; any one of those travelling lights could bring the aircraft down. They were still in front and from this distance it didn't seem necessary to climb higher to keep above them. The main worry was fighters. No searchlights yet.

'Coming up to the target.' Plover's voice wasn't quite as calm now; he was speaking a little louder, a little faster. 'Right a bit.' Pause. 'A bit more. Too much – left.'

Pause. 'Just like that. Hold it.' If the engines suddenly cut there would still be silence.

Plover's voice made Mason start as he yelled excitedly, 'Right a bit! Right a bit … damn and blast. Round again. Sorry.'

No need for Plover to be sorry. This was his first serious bomb-aiming attempt. 'Don't worry, cock. This is a little different to a bombing range back home', Mason told him.

Wood came in: 'If you don't get in next time, though, I'll have your guts for garters.'

It was fascinating looking straight down at the flak coming up. When you picked out one tracer shell as it left the ground, it seemed to be travelling very slowly, heading directly for the aircraft, and then just when it seemed that it couldn't miss, it veered off at an incredible speed and disappeared, quicker than the eye could follow. Looking straight down it was impossible not to pick out one particular shell and follow it, and it was difficult to believe that they would all veer off before they reached the aircraft.

Over the sea, Mason swung the machine to the left this time, so that banking round he could examine the target area. Most of the guns had stopped firing, leaving one or two still optimistically raking the sky. With what object he didn't know, because they were a mile off and there were no other aircraft on the same target that night. He held the aircraft in a wide bank, keeping the docks in sight all the time, until several miles behind the town he pulled her round a bit more to head for the target, then straightened out for the next run-in. Almost immediately the guns opened up again. The nose of the aircraft hid the target now and it was up to Plover.

'Keep like that', Plover said. 'Steady as she goes.' Plover was being flippant for the sake of something to say. 'Right a bit … a bit more … hold it … hold it …' With frightening suddenness a searchlight stabbed the sky a little to their left, then another on the right.

'Searchlights behind.' That was Drake in the tail. Must be some more at the back. The two on either side had now joined up out in front, a little too high, then a third joined them from somewhere behind.

'Hold her steady. Just coming up.' Plover's voice reminded Mason they were on a bombing run. Although the lights hadn't found them yet, it seemed awfully bright up there. He wished Plover would hurry up. Any moment those lights …

'Bombs gone!'

The relief of hearing those words did not last long. At almost the same time one of the lights broke away from the cone, swung towards them and swept the aircraft with a fierce glare. Then another, but this one caught them and held them. In a matter of seconds they were held fast in a cone of dazzling brightness. The engines screamed and everything was vibrating, as with nose down and full throttle the aircraft headed out to sea. Any moment Mason expected fighter bullets to come tearing into them. They were down to two thousand feet and well over the sea, but still the lights held them. A risk had to be taken with the flak but they were out of range now. Several miles later and at fifteen hundred feet one of the lights gave up, and shortly after another, leaving just one still on them. Not long after, at the extremity of its power, this too went out, and they were left in blessed darkness once more.

Mason straightened out and relaxed in his seat, glancing at Wood. Wood leant back too and grinned, making a brow-mopping gesture. 'Op Number One', he said into the intercom.

Drake's voice said, 'Number One? We haven't got to do any more, have we?'

IV

Just over the hedge on his right Mason passed the next machine – 'J for Johnnie'. The bomb doors were open and the bombs were being hauled up. A thousand pounder and some five hundreds. One mechanic was chalking something on the thousand pounder and the others were laughing – something rude about Hitler, no doubt.

Mason couldn't see his own machine; it was over on the far side. 'G for George'. He'd never done a trip in her, only a flying test, and wondered if the fact that he didn't like the machine was really a premonition. Would somebody be saying tomorrow, 'Funny, you know, old Mason seemed to have a feeling he wasn't coming back last night. He was fussing like hell about his aircraft.' He knew perfectly well why he didn't like the machine. It was a small point, he told himself, but it had been working on him all day, ever since he had been told this morning that 'G for George' was to be his aircraft for tonight. He'd watched her land a couple of days ago and noticed she had a Glycol leak. The whole of one side was covered with this evil-smelling cooling liquid. It was not flammable, Mason kept telling himself, and didn't mean a thing. But it was not right and if that was wrong there might be other things wrong – little things as though somebody was trying to warn you. He didn't really believe in this psychic business, but he wished he wasn't going in 'G for George'.

The aircraft needed a splash or two of paint too. This afternoon after landing from the flying test he'd walked round her – she was still leaking Glycol, though not so badly perhaps – and noticed a number of spots where the black anti-flash paint had chipped off from the belly. The gleaming silver metal was shining through. He wondered at the time if it would be sufficient to pick up the glare of searchlights and lead fighters and flak onto him. He wanted to tell the ground crew to patch it, but they might have laughed behind his back and related the story in their billets.

Mason had a feeling that others were beginning to notice that he was scared. The Sergeant parachute-packer had looked at him in a peculiar way this morning when he'd taken his 'chute in for re-packing. It had been done only a week before and the order said once a month. But he'd been sitting on it and that might have creased the silk or tangled the cords, somehow. Anyway, he'd lent it to Simpson yesterday when he couldn't find the key of his locker and didn't want to force the door. Simpson could have played football with it for all he knew.

Most people seemed not to bother about their 'chutes, even when they were squashed quite flat. Some would leave them lying around the crew-room for anybody to use as a cushion or foot-rest, and never bothered about getting them re-packed until they were told to.

Rather odd, that; they were such important things and it took very little effort to walk along to the Parachute Section. Mason didn't believe in taking any chances, no matter how small. That small chance might make all the difference one day.

Only once had he taken a chance and that had taught him a lesson. At the time the fact that the air-speed indicator wasn't working properly didn't seem important, on a routine flight in cloudless weather. Just as he was getting into the aircraft he remembered not having reported the defect after the last flight, and after a moment's hesitation decided he was being fussy, and took off. It was a cold day, but beautiful, with the sun sparkling on the snow-covered countryside, and everything was going fine, except for the air-speed indicator, which was wavering about a bit when it should have been constant. After a while it appeared to be getting worse, and a little later he could see that it definitely was worse. By the time they got back over the aerodrome it was useless, the needle floating from one side of the dial to the other.

Mason had landed a machine without that indicator, and crossing the perimeter, near enough to the ground to get perspective, knew that he was coming in much too fast. Out of the corner of his eye he saw Wood turn from the window and look at him, then at the instrument panel, and back to him again. He gave Wood what he hoped was a reassuring nod, trying to incorporate in that nod an indication that he was going to land, and not go round again. Better to risk a fast landing than a stall,

51

by pulling the nose up without an A.S.I. It was too late now anyway. When he closed the throttles, a few feet off the ground, Mason could see he was too far over the field to avoid running across the perimeter track onto the rough ground beyond. The snow was crisp and the brakes were more of a danger than a help. The wheels touched, crunching the snow, and the machine reared up, while he fought to hold her steady, waiting for the next bounce. The undercarriage thudded once more and she lifted a little, touched again, bumpily, and settled, running fast. Wood shouted something, pointing ahead, but Mason had already seen it. The long, low wall of frozen snow from the cleared perimeter track was about two feet high and they were going to hit it. There was just time to yell 'Brace yourselves' to the crew, who were probably already doing that anyway, before the wheels hit the mound of hard snow and the aircraft leapt into the air, wallowing crazily. Control of the aircraft had gone and there was nothing to do but wait for it. Wood sat on the floor, bracing his legs and back, and Long, who had left his radio desk when they first touched down, thinking they were now safe, quickly did the same.

She landed beautifully. Heavily, but fair and square on the undercarriage, on reasonably even ground, and came to rest a few yards from the boundary hedge.

Nobody moved, and after a moment or two Mason revved the engines, closed the throttles and switched off. His forehead felt clammy and uncomfortable and he took his helmet off as the props whistled to a stop. Wood and

Long got to their feet, taking their helmets off. Long said 'Jesus!' and grinned at Pepper who had emerged from the front turret. It was Pepper's first flight on the squadron – he'd arrived a couple of days before and had taken Plover's place as second pilot when Plover had been made captain. 'Is the initiation ceremony over?' he grinned. 'If so, can I get out?'

There was the usual ragging for several days, from the Squadron Leader downwards, but that was all because there had been no damage. But there could have been. It might have been fatal – for all of them – and the blame would have been directly his. All through taking a chance, and a small one at that.

That was way back last year, though, and Mason had learnt a lot since then. The longer you lasted, the fewer chances you could afford to take because of the law of averages. He'd kept going for a long time now – anyway, longer than anybody on the station, so he couldn't afford to take any at all.

All the same, he couldn't stand being laughed at over it. Surely it was no laughing matter to take all the precautions you possibly could?

Of course, the main trouble with these chaps who laughed at his fussiness was that they didn't realise they were, in all probability, going to get killed. It was the others, they thought, not them, who would be killed. They didn't seem to understand that it was only the lucky ones, who had also taken no chances, who had a hope of getting through. They didn't know anything about Wright, Pepper, Trewsom, Barclay, Mills, Dwyer, Coleman, Pope, Marples and all the others who had gone. To them they weren't even names. To Mason they were people, each name recalling vivid memories of episodes, experiences, small incidents – some pleasant, some unpleasant, but to him all seeming very real, still. Before their time. They only knew of the few who went for a burton before they themselves went down. They hadn't been, for nine months, watching one after the other go, sometimes so soon after arriving on the station that he didn't get to know their names. They didn't know of the chap whose kit was sent off to his next of kin, still unpacked, the day after he'd arrived. They didn't know about Smith, who had come up to Mason in the mess one day, two days after joining the squadron, pulled up a chair, and said, 'You on tonight?'

'Yes', he'd answered. 'Are you?' Although Mason could see that he was.

'My first trip', Smith said, one hand scratching an ear and the other fiddling with his belt-buckle, grinning, embarrassed.

Mason knew Smith was going to ask him what it was like. How he hated that. What could you tell these first-trippers? That it was bloody awful, frightening, sickeningly so, and more often fatal? That each trip got worse? That each time you got back you could hardly believe it? That the ground seemed so solid and firm and friendly and you were just about to feel happy when you realised that it only meant you were alive to go again, and again, and then again, until God knows when? That if you lasted long enough you became lonely because all your friends had gone? That you got into such a state that you had to suppress all your emotions, like anger, sentimentality, soft-heartedness, even gratitude and kindness, and certainly fear, because it made your lip quiver and you wanted to cry?

'What's it like?' Smith said.

'Oh, not so bad. A bit shaky sometimes. Some are worse than others.'

Smith relaxed a little. It was just the belt-buckle now. 'Have you done Berlin before?' he asked.

'No, I haven't. It'll be my first trip there too.' Mason wished Smith would stop, but felt sorry for him because he was excited and nervous and being a stranger had no one to talk to. Trying to veer off the subject, he asked Smith, 'Who are you flying with tonight?'

'Pepper. I'm going second pilot, of course.'

Pepper had only done a few trips himself – couldn't have been more than a couple of weeks on the squadron. 'Oh, Pepper, he's all right. He did his first trip with me. Care for a drink?'

But Smith's mind was on the first trip tonight and he brought the subject back with, 'They tell me that once you get over the first three you don't mind it'.

'Yes, I've heard them say that. Of course, people react in different ways. Let's get over to the bar.'

They rose, and on the way to the bar Smith continued, 'What were your first three like?'

'Oh, I don't know.' Mason didn't mean to sound off-hand, just wanted to change the subject. 'My first two or three were fairly easy, I think. What will you have?'

A week later Smith was dead. His third trip. Came down in the sea on the way back, they heard.

It was Bill Bailey who told him. 'Not bad, eh, for three trips?', said Bill. 'Crashed on the first, baled out on the second and killed on the third.'

Then Mason told Bill about that conversation, and said, 'I wonder what he thought as he was going down?'

'Oh', Bill had remarked, with his hard intolerant smile, 'he probably thought, "Thank Christ for that – I'll be used to it after this".'

No, these men didn't know about chaps like Smith.

Nor, for that matter, chaps like Bill Bailey. Bitter, cynical Bill, an intellectual, an atheist, who, on hearing that Trewsom, of the huge ginger moustache, had been seen to go down with his aircraft a mass of flames, had merely grunted and said, 'I bet that singed his whiskers'.

Mason would have liked to see old Bill again. They'd had some good times together in the old days. Getting on all right apparently in Training Command, according to his last letter. 'Dear Cock', he wrote, 'shocking machines we've got here. Mine caught fire in the air the other day. I was the cool instructor until we landed and then I ran like buggery. The pupils loved it, bless their little hearts.'

Bill never did understand why he'd been posted after only 21 trips, and thought it was because of his eyes. Quite likely it was, but it might have been because he was by far the finest, coolest pilot on the squadron and good pilots were valuable, particularly as instructors. Bill never left anything to chance. He used to attend every lecture going, and would quite often baffle the lecturer – remorselessly. He had no time for incompetence. In fact he would be very useful in Training Command.

V

Mason had skirted the aerodrome and was now at the
main gate. He wondered what he could do now, where
he could go. They weren't taking off till 10.30. There
was a dance on in the mess tonight but there was no
point in going yet because it wouldn't have started. Not
that he was going to dance anyway. There wouldn't be
anybody there he knew, and none of the aircrew chaps
would have invited anybody, obviously. Still, he'd go
along later and watch these people dancing and jig-
ging around. He would probably be over the target at
the time they were bidding lurching 'goodnights' on
the way to their homes and beds. In the morning they
would chatter about what a nice time they'd had and
look forward to the next one. What would he be doing
tomorrow? Assuming that he got back, he wouldn't be
able to look forward to the next dance. Couldn't look
forward to anything. Except leave perhaps. He always
looked forward to leave, but when he was actually on
leave it was an effort to enjoy himself. Lots of drinks, a
couple of dates with girls he couldn't get interested in,
a film or two. The family wanting to know all about his
ops. His mother asking why he didn't bring a chap or
two home, and why not do it next leave.

When Mason was on leave he always used to think how much better it would be if you could have all your leave at the end instead of in odd bits and pieces, which only seemed to drag out the time. What he wanted to know was whether or not he was going to get through his ops. Going on leave didn't help. It only meant he had to wait longer to find out.

No point in going to the mess yet. He'd go down to the locker-room and make sure all his gear was there. Just as well, in case somebody had borrowed something, as on the last occasion when Barclay had borrowed his helmet and forgotten to put it back. Mason couldn't stand those last-minute flaps. It was the sort of thing they talked about when an aircraft didn't come back.

He wouldn't wear much flying kit tonight – just helmet, jersey and boots, and gloves, of course. It was always his hands that suffered from the cold. He couldn't remember who it was who had given him that tip about covering up the wrists. It worked well. By wrapping up his wrists he found he could leave off his woollen gloves and just wear the silk ones. It left the fingers that much freer in case you wanted to do anything quickly, like manipulating the catch on the escape hatch, or clipping on a parachute.

Mason remembered the time when he and Ken were on a training flight and thought they would have to bale out over the Scottish mountains. They both spent what seemed an age fiddling and struggling with their 'chute harness, getting their fingers caught up in the oxygen and intercom cables dangling from their helmets. In his excitement Ken had put his 'chute on upside down, and when later they landed safely they had both been helpless with laughter. The funniest part of the incident, though, was when Ken discovered that the book he had grabbed at random off the crew-room table, to read when it was his turn to relax, was called *Fatal Friday*. It had been particularly funny because it happened to be a Friday.

It made him sad to remember Ken, leaning back in his seat, his head thrown back, laughing as though he would never stop.

It was rather peculiar that he and Ken should have been so much alike. After all, their friendship had only developed because their names both happened to begin with 'M', and consequently they were always paired off on the exercise lists. 'K. Minty and L. Mason', the instructor had announced that day way back, 'low level flying – "K for King", 9.30. J. Curtis and S. Cole, same machine – 11 o'clock.' 'K for King' had gone down in the sea on that 11 o'clock exercise. An engine cut at sea level. That evening, walking along the sea-front, Mason had watched an RAF launch and a couple of motor boats searching for their bodies. Curtis and Cole were the first to go, and in one gigantic stride the possibility was brought nearer.

He wouldn't have felt so bad about it, he thought, if he hadn't had the letter from Roger's wife that morning saying that Roger was reported missing. It had been a shock to him because he didn't know Roger had been sent to Norway.

Roger had been so proud of having shot down a Dornier flying boat the last time he'd seen him. That was at the wedding. Nice girl, Veronica – Von, as they called her. It was funny she hadn't written to him again. She knew what great friends he and Roger had been, right from their earliest school days.

Those summer holidays seemed so far away now. They had never got tired of the same camp site – year after year, at every opportunity, they went to the same place. He supposed they both liked the place because they were so keen on swimming. They spent as much time in the river as they did on land. On cold days they used to have a fire outside the tent, and always in the evenings, of course. Dusk was the best time, he thought – pulling on warm sweaters as the evening got chilly, putting more wood on the fire and then cooking supper. It was usually sausages or fish with great wads of bread and butter. Then, usually, came 'Melody Time', both trying to sing the popular songs of the day in harmony. Neither could sing and this led to many an argument as to who had caused a particularly offensive discord. Tiring of that, they would loll about round the fire. It must have been a very great friendship because he couldn't remember what they talked about.

One year, their last year at school, they'd asked the Harvey twins along. But the Harvey boys seemed much keener on talking about girls than on swimming, collecting wood or going for water; and when they packed up and left before they had intended to, he and Roger had been glad. They never asked anybody after that. Not that there was much camping after that because they both left school and went to work, and could only manage short weekends and the two weeks' summer holidays.

The camping holidays drifted after that. They were both sorry about it and always intended one day to arrange another holiday in the same field by the same deserted river. Then war came, Roger got married, and now he was dead. Somewhere off Norway. They hadn't even found his body.

There was nobody in the locker-room when Mason got there. He was glad of that because it would only have meant a lot of silly chatter. In any case there were ghosts in there and these other chaps didn't seem to fit in. He still, for instance, thought of the lockers by the names of those who had them when he first arrived. The locker next to his would always be 'Minty's locker', and the one on the other side, 'Plover's'. It had never occurred to him to refer to them in any other way, and now, for the first time, he realised how odd it must have sounded to the others. He should, he supposed, get out of the habit. If there was time, of course. That was just it – it didn't seem worthwhile altering or changing anything, because of the time.

Mason looked at Ken's locker. 'J. Harper' was chalked on the door. That was the tall, fair bloke with the silly smile. He hadn't liked the way Harper had sort of taken over the locker, as though it had been specially put there for him. Harper didn't seem to realise that at least two others had had that locker, even after Ken, whose locker it really was.

'Ah, you're my neighbour, are you?' Harper had said, rather too loudly, the day he arrived, while he shoved his almost unworn flying kit into the locker, grinning like a fool.

Mason hoped he wouldn't grin like that tonight. This morning, as the Flight Commander had started to read out the crew list, he had had a feeling that Harper was going with him tonight. As their names were read out Harper looked across at him, grinning that stupid bloody grin. Anybody would think they were taking part in a boat race or something. Looking at Harper as Harper turned away, Mason thought to himself, 'He's the sort who will panic if we get into trouble'. You could tell them; there was something about their looks and manner. Like Swann – he'd had those same pale eyes that moved before the head turned, that same pretty skin and the loose meaningless grin. Swann didn't do much grinning that night over Kiel, though. That was the first trip with Mason's present crew.

Watching Harper, Mason thought of Swann, standing up in the cabin, half-crouched and sort of rigid. Mason had never seen anybody paralysed with fear before, and hoped he wouldn't again. The sight of that moist grey face, like wet clay, and the horribly staring eyes would always be clear in his mind. And those white knuckles gripping the ledge running along the top of the instrument panel as though they were bolted to it – a transparent white, the bones almost bursting through. Swann had never done a Kiel trip before and on the first bombing run was obviously aghast at the amount of flak the Germans could put up on a really worthwhile target. Tomlinson was doing the bomb-aiming this trip and Swann's job as second pilot was to stand by and take over the aircraft if necessary. The flak was so heavy it was difficult to get a clean run-in, and on the fifth one, when something burst through the side of the cabin and out through the roof, Swann began to show signs of giving way. Jerking a look at the jagged hole in the roof, he went down on one knee, his body arched and his head well down, below window level. For some reason he took his gloves off. He stayed like that for the whole of the circuit and during the next run-in. Even Tomlinson's 'Bombs gone' didn't stir him. There wasn't much time to worry about him after that. Diving through the confusion of flak thumping all round them, the glare of the lights as though they were shining into the aircraft from a few yards' distance, the smell of cordite scooped up as they flew through the smoke of exploded shells, Holt's voice yelled urgently, 'Fire! A flare's been hit'. Within seconds Tomlinson was out of the front turret, and after one quick glance at Swann, who had suddenly risen and was now gripping the panel ledge, staring ahead, pushed past him and went to Holt's assistance.

Dent wouldn't leave the rear turret until he was told, Mason knew, and just as he was about to call him up, Dent came through: 'Shall I give a hand, skipper?'

'Yes', he told him, 'but if you think they can manage, get back. And Dent, report the damage.' It was horrible not knowing what was going on behind there, and Tomlinson and Holt had to unplug their intercom when they left their positions. Swann was still motionless. The flak was easing off a little, perhaps, but each shell was as dangerous as the others, no matter how many or few there were, and they were still in the lights. If the flak stopped there'd be fighters. Then Dent would be needed – where the hell was he? Perhaps that fire in the fuselage was getting a hold. Perhaps the aircraft had already started to burn before Holt called up. Mason began to wonder what he'd do with Swann if they had to bale out. Didn't know how he would react. To test him he tried to knock those knuckles off the ledge, but they were solid. Then, at the third knock, Swann slowly turned his head, looking blankly around with staring eyes. Taking one hand off the controls Mason gripped Swann's arm and pulled him down. The flak had stopped – where was Dent? With his free hand he wrenched at the oxygen mask clip on Swann's helmet and ripped the mask off. In the white glare of the lights Swann's lips were a peculiar colour and his tongue was visible.

Dent's voice: 'All right, skipper. We bunged it out of the hatch. Tommy and Holt are making sure. There's a hole burnt through to the bomb bay.'

'Thanks, Dent. Nice work. Keep a look out.' An unnecessary remark but the sort of thing one said on those occasions, and Dent understood. 'Right', he said.

They were down to four thousand feet when the lights, first one, then the others – however many there were – swung off them, presumably onto a more vulnerable target.

Tomlinson crawled through the aperture from the fusclage, gave thumbs-up as he came into the cabin, then nodded enquiringly towards Swann. There was no need to tell him that Swann was not manageable, and Tomlinson pulled him with no great ceremony into the co-pilot's seat. Swann didn't resist. He just sat there, dazed, his lower lip working, his morale completely gone. Tomlinson crouched on the floor, took the maps on his bent knees, and began working out the course home.

When they got back from that trip, Mason had suggested to the rest of the crew that the incident should be reported to the C.O. and they agreed. Nobody could blame them. Why should they? Swann was now doing some safe flying job somewhere or other and they were still doing ops. Swann certainly wouldn't blame them. He'd be laughing like mad, bragging about his ops in an area where nobody could check up on him.

Mason could just imagine Harper acting like Swann. Whether on ops or in the local pubs and cafés or at dances. Very brave and gay with the girls, charming to the older people who asked him questions about flying over Germany, side-stepping any embarrassing question with a laughing-cum-serious 'Even walls have ears, you know'. And fellows like Roger and Ken were dead. They had been frightened too – but they had been frightened all the time, not only when they saw, heard and smelt the flak.

It wasn't so much that he didn't like Harper, really – he just had no time for him. Couldn't be bothered with his type. He could easily get to dislike him, though, if Harper got in his way, and he would get in his way if they were thrown together too much – like being in the same crew.

Mason opened his locker and something fell out. Something always fell out when he opened his locker. He often wondered why its untidiness never irritated him. Even when he was trying to find something and had to pull everything out onto the floor, it didn't anger him as it did a lot of chaps. Perhaps it was because they would really like to keep their lockers tidy, whereas he didn't care. He was always coming across fellows 'tidying up' their lockers and a couple of days later they would be just as bad.

He looked at his now. Untidy maybe, but all the things he was likely to want were either at the front or on the top, except for one glove, which was on the floor. It was quite true he wouldn't be able to get out his flying jacket without removing all the other things first, but it was summer now and he didn't use it often. If he did he'd have some other arrangement.

Nothing to lose your temper about, like Simpson this morning – standing there with half the contents of his locker round his feet, tugging at his intercom cable which had got caught up, muttering angrily, 'Come out, you … These are bloody silly lockers. Not nearly big enough.'

Mason liked Simpson. He had those funny shaped eyebrows that made him look perpetually worried. And enormous feet. He was always grumbling but his grumbles usually ended in an easy laugh. One of his main grumbles was his forage cap. He could never keep it on because his head was a peculiar shape, and his hair was thick, wiry and quite uncontrollable, seeming to grow upwards and sideways according to the shape of his head. He never minded jokes about his hair and cap, in fact he usually let the jokes pass.

Simpson was a good pilot too, in spite of his apparent slap-happiness. Although only a comparative newcomer to the squadron, he had quite a few trips to his credit, including the one after which he was called upon to give a lecture to the rest of the squadron on how he brought back his aircraft in a condition which defied all known laws of aeronautics.

'I don't really deserve any credit', Simpson began modestly, when the room had quietened sufficiently for him to make himself heard. 'All the credit is due to my instructor – Arch Marshal of the Royal Air Force, Sir Selph Preservation'. He had struck just the right note and everybody roared.

It would be a pity if Simpson got killed because he would make a good citizen in civvy street. And there was a girl too. She lived in the town and they had only known each other for a short while, but whenever you met him, or whenever he turned up by arrangement, she was always with him. They never showed any signs of affection between them, but you could tell. Extremely attractive girl – jet black hair, a nice figure and a lovely smile.

What would happen there? Would Simpson eventually be posted and keep in touch with her, and marry her one day? Or would he be killed? It could happen any day and she wouldn't know anything about it until he failed to turn up at their next date. Next of kin would of course be immediately informed by the Padre, the Adjutant, or the C.O. But who would know about this girl, waiting somewhere? Or care.

After waiting a while she would become a little worried because he had never done this before, and she knew he wouldn't if he could help it. Allowing him perhaps another ten minutes she would decide to risk the remarks passed in the mess, and phone him. If the person at the other end recognised her, or guessed who she was, he would probably say, 'Vic Simpson? Just a minute', and go and fetch Sammy. It wasn't the duty of the mess steward to deal with these matters, but nobody could do the job better than old Sammy. He seemed to have automatically accepted the job, and in turn to have been automatically accepted by the chaps. During a busy spell of ops such as they were having now, Sammy would be called to the phone quite often, and those standing at the bar would hear his sympathetic, fatherly voice say, 'I'm afraid he's not here. Who is calling please?' He would listen carefully to the name and then might say, 'Was he expecting you to call?'

The answer to that question and the tone in which it was given would tell Sammy all he wanted to know. He would then go on, with various degrees of gentleness and sympathy, according to how he'd sized up the situation, and break the news, explaining why there would be no other news for at least four weeks. More often than not he would be heard to take the girl's name and address and promise to notify her as soon as anything came through. And he would.

Those at the bar would be glad when the conversation was over and they could get back to normal.

Whenever Mason was at the bar and heard Sammy coping with that sort of phone call, he would always try to form a mental picture of the girl at the other end. Would she be crying? Or dazed? Or both? In all probability she wouldn't know the missing bloke's parents, or even his home address. One didn't prepare for this sort of thing. None of his effects would be sent to her, and she would receive no official notification. Her one link would be the mess steward, but neither of them would have known of each other's existence if this hadn't occurred. In any case, the mess steward might leave the station and that last link would be broken. If her feelings for the chap who was missing were sincere she would feel very lonely, cut off. But, of course, she might not be the sincere type. She might be the light-hearted, fluffy, melodramatic sort, getting quite a kick out of it, already imagining herself telling her friends. Trying to decide whether to make it appear the tragedy of her life, or whether to profess a sense of guilt because she hadn't had the same feelings for him as he'd had for her. Even perhaps trying to suggest that he may have done it deliberately, or at any rate that he hadn't had much desire to come back.

Simpson's girlfriend wouldn't be like that, though – she was definitely sincere. It would be a great pity if he got killed.

VI

Everything Mason needed for tonight was there. There was nothing to do now but kill time in the mess until about ten.

Closing the locker door he walked out, but instead of making for the mess he turned left through the main doors onto the tarmac and stood looking out across the aerodrome. It was deserted now. All the aircraft were ready and the ground staff had gone off for supper. They would be back about ten too.

It was a lovely evening and war was a long way off. Everything was so quiet. So innocently peaceful. Looking across the green fields, the still trees, to the purple tinge of the Pennine hills in the distance, listening to the sounds of the countryside that only a listener could hear, the distant shout of a cowman, the lowing of his herd, the bark of his dog, Mason began to wonder, all over again, what it was all about. Why was he leaving this scene in a few hours' time to challenge man's defences with man's weapons, to destroy or be destroyed? Was defeat more bitter than death, was death sweeter than defeat? He supposed so, but he didn't at this moment really understand it, because death could be achieved any time, in dozens of ways – if defeat was so bad – without taking the lives of others. Living was the difficulty, not dying. Anyway, what was victory without life? A stone memorial, one name amongst many, read occasionally by a casual stroller or somebody waiting for a bus?

Mason pushed these thoughts away and brought his mind back to material facts. The aircraft dispersed all round the airfield were ready for tonight. He still couldn't see 'G for George'. The field dipped in that corner.

He wished he still had his bike – he would have gone over, just to have a look round. You could examine things more closely when there was nobody about.

Confound Wood. If it hadn't been for him he would still have his bike. Wood hadn't asked if he could borrow the thing either. Not that there was anything unusual in that, in the ordinary way, but he must have realised on that occasion that anybody with a bike there would have used it. Whenever an aircraft had a mishap of any kind it was natural for everybody to go over and have a look, or to give a hand if necessary. Those with bikes would obviously want them. And of all the damn silly things to do – resting the bike against the undercarriage wheel, after a landing like that. You could see from the hangar by the way the machine was lying, half in and half out of the gun emplacement, that the undercarriage was going to collapse sideways any minute.

Because Mason was balancing on top of a ladder fixing the radio aerial when Simpson yelled through the door, 'Wright's in a bunker', he was a long way behind the others as they rushed out of the crew-room. When

he found his bike missing he guessed somebody had borrowed it, and walked over. By the time he got there the
undercarriage had collapsed and everybody was shouting
advice. The ambulance, which with the fire tender had
been first on the scene, was speeding towards the sick bay.

It was a hot day, and partly because he was so hot and
sticky and partly because he'd missed the actual collapse,
Mason had been decidedly bad-tempered.

'Who the hell's pinched my bloody bike?' he yelled
as soon as he was within shouting distance.

Wood walked towards him. 'I'm sorry, old boy, I
didn't know it was yours', he said, as though that made
it all right.

'Well it is mine. And ask another time.' (Stupid really,
because if Wood had asked, he wouldn't have lent it to
him, obviously.) 'Where is it now?'

Wood started to mutter something as they reached
the wrecked machine but stopped as everybody began
to titter and giggle. Then Wood began to snigger. That
should have made Mason really angry, but Wood was
a likeable fool and was laughing against his will, like a
schoolboy guilty of a prank gone wrong and smother-
ing his own mirth to avoid capitulation. Glaring from
Wood round to the others, Mason said something like,
'What's so funny about a bloke having his bike pinched?'
Then a suspicion began to dawn on him that there *was*
something funny about it, and turning back to Wood he
said, 'Well, come on – where is it?' Wood waved vaguely
at the aircraft. Mason still couldn't see it. 'I can't see

the bloody thing. Where ...' Then he did see it – just. It was lying under one of the engines, crushed, broken, and completely useless.

There were a few facetious remarks but in general the joke had passed.

'You bastard', said Mason, and Wood mumbled something about 'getting him another one'.

'You'd better.'

But in the mess that night, his annoyance gone, Mason told Wood not to be a fool – he didn't want another one.

'Drinks on Wood all round', somebody shouted, and Wood ordered up cheerfully.

It had been tough luck on Plover, who had been in the nose of the aircraft and the only one hurt. His injuries had not been considered serious and they were all surprised to learn two days later that he'd died, and all because, apparently, he hadn't urinated before he landed. The Doc the next day gave them a lecture and explained how Plover had had a clout in the guts, but would have been all right if his bladder hadn't burst. From then on they were all ordered to land with empty bladders, and somebody asked if it was advisable to take precautions against a clout in the back, and Simpson said he always did take those precautions anyway – usually in the target area. Altogether it had been a very amusing lecture. Mason remembered how the room had been silent only when Plover's name was mentioned. If you didn't mention names it was just some vague person who had been killed, sort of remote and nowhere near you. If you mentioned names it made you realise it could have been you.

That must be the reason why nobody mentioned fellows who had gone. Mason had been aware for a long time that he didn't like talking about them, and had noticed that there were others, older hands, who apparently felt the same. That was why, of course.

'You know', Bailey had once said in his quick, intense way, one night in The Unicorn, 'I read in a book once that it's just as though they've stepped behind a mirror. I think it's a perfect description, don't you?'

Actually he didn't, but Mason agreed with Bill, because it was near enough. Ken had been there too but at the time was busy trying to get a girl sitting in the corner to show some signs of encouragement.

'Don't you think so, Ken?' Bill asked, and seeing the look of concentration on Ken's face followed his eyes to the corner. 'I say, that's rather nice.'

They all three stared at the poor girl, muttering and grunting their approval, just in time to receive a furious glare from the fellow who had suddenly returned to her, an aggressive-looking Army major with a brushed-up moustache.

'Ah, yes, mirrors', Ken said elaborately, turning back to the bar. 'What about them?' But the conversation was over, and Bill made him buy a drink out of turn for nearly getting them all into trouble.

Neither Bill nor Ken had been at that lecture about Plover, though. Not that it would have helped Ken, and

Bill probably wouldn't have learnt anything from it anyway.

The silence out there on the tarmac, and his thoughts, were interrupted by the sound of footsteps coming round the corner, so Mason started walking in the opposite direction, turning his head as he went. It was the Flight Sergeant Mechanic, probably just going off duty, having seen that everything was ready for tonight. He was glad he hadn't waited because he didn't like the chap. Never had done since he'd heard him talking to another fellow about the crash that had killed Ken. Apparently it had been most inconvenient to have been dragged out of bed at four in the morning, all because somebody couldn't fly an aircraft properly. Also the smell caused by the three who had been burnt to death had upset his stomach – made him feel quite sick and he couldn't eat his break-fast. Horrible it was, what with the cold and everything. The other fellow had been most sympathetic because he'd had a similar experience and knew what it was like. A shocking smell, couldn't get it out of your clothes.

Sitting in the mess, overhearing that conversation, Mason had felt a terrific surge of anger, but managed to control himself sufficiently to stand up and speak to them.

'You two want to get your feet off the ground, then somebody else will have to put up with the smell.' They stared at him in surprise as he turned and stalked away.

Thinking it over outside, when he'd cooled down a little, it wasn't a particularly good remark he'd made and he could think of many things far more biting. That had made him angry again, and he'd gone back into the mess intending to re-open the conversation but they had both gone. Couldn't remember who the other fellow had been now – never seen him before, or since. Somebody just passing through, perhaps. Mason had only spoken to the Flight Sergeant once since then and he'd made him angry again. It had been more or less for the same reason, but this time he'd been just plain angry, without the additional agitation because it wasn't Ken he was talking about.

Reporting back from hospital, Mason had gone to the Squadron Leader's office and found, instead, this Flight Sergeant sitting there. He thought that was a cheek, to start with.

'Where's Squadron Leader Barry?'

The Flight Sergeant had looked at him in genuine surprise for a moment before resuming his irritating superior manner.

'Oh, he went for a burton.' As he said it, he sort of waved his hand in a kind of dismissal, and continued to read a paper in front of him. Whether the Flight Sergeant was trying to dismiss him or just dismissing the fact that Barry and four others had been wiped out, Mason didn't know, but whatever it was, that sudden white-hot anger, which he didn't remember having before the war, rushed through his chest to his head. It was difficult to keep to the subject.

'When was this? I've been in hospital since that crash

three weeks ago. Remember?' Mason tried to make that 'remember' sound as nasty as possible, and could see that the Flight Sergeant realised it. It was gratifying to recall that he looked decidedly uncomfortable as he shuffled some papers about, because a faulty engine had been partly to blame.

'A week or so ago.'

'Who's commanding now?'

'A new chap – Squadron Leader Bantock.'

Mason walked out of the office, deliberately leaving the door open, and went to the mess, where he saw Barrett.

Barrett was sitting in an armchair reading a magazine, and he sat next to him. 'Hello', Barrett said, laying the magazine on his lap, politely pleasant. 'Are you all right now?'

'Yes, thanks. It was nothing much.' It was nice of Barrett, but he wanted to know about Barry. 'What happened to Barry?'

'Emden, about a week ago. We went there two nights running and he got it the second night.'

'Any chance, do you think?'

Barrett didn't like talking about blokes not coming back but was being understandingly tolerant. 'No', he said, 'no chance at all. A Blenheim went down that night too, and according to reports it looks as though they collided.'

'Whose reports?' (Mason couldn't help it – he wanted to know about Barry.)

'Well, we had four on that night and took over from the Blenheims. Milsom was just arriving when he and his crew saw an explosion and what looked like two machines going down on fire. Milsom took off number two, following Barry. The Blenheim boys reported one missing and one of their chaps said the same thing.'

It was clear that Barrett considered he had now given all the information possible. Anyway, this was old stuff, and a lot had happened since then.

'Well', Mason said to Barrett, as he saw his eyes wander to the magazine on his lap, 'thanks for the gen. I'd better go and get the chickens out of my room.'

He remembered going to his room and sitting on the bed. Going to his room during the daytime was not a thing Mason normally did, but on this occasion there didn't seem to be anywhere else to go. He was shaken about Barry. He really had thought that Barry stood a greater chance than most of getting through. He had been the take-no-chance type, always telling the blokes to pay attention at briefing, study the target map, report any defect in the aircraft, because the object was to get there and back.

They'd been quite friendly, in a way. As friendly as a Sergeant and a Squadron Leader could be anyway. Mason had got to know him pretty well when they'd both gone to fetch that new aircraft.

The aircraft hadn't been ready and they spent three days waiting for it, in a hotel in the town because it was a civilian aerodrome and had no accommodation. Most of the time they spent drinking and soon found they had a lot in common. Barry was scared too, and consequently took his operation flying seriously.

They had discussed the business of finding some reason for putting off doing ops, even when you knew you were getting out of nothing – you still had to do them afterwards. It was only playing for time. You wanted to get on with your ops, they both agreed, as quickly as possible so that you could find out if you were going to get through. In fact you wanted to speed up the war – ops every day, every night, one after the other – finish the war quickly, so there'd be no more to do.

But at the same time, when an opportunity of missing a trip or two presented itself, you grabbed it with both hands. No doubt, they decided, it was because if you missed a trip you were sure of at least one more day, whereas that one trip might have been your last. Not that you could really enjoy that day, even by being blind drunk. It was just clinging to life.

It had been on the last evening that they reached that stage. They had both been pretty drunk and had dreadful hangovers the next day, only to find on reporting to the airfield that the aircraft was ready. It was a wild, gusty day, and the aircraft was going to bump a lot.

'Christ', Barry said, 'I'll be as sick as a dog.'

'So will I', Mason told Barry, 'so don't hog the Elsan pan or there'll be a nice mess in this beautiful new aircraft.'

Barry hadn't been sick, though – but Mason had.

When they landed, Barry found him lying beside the Elsan pan. 'Who's hogging the Elsan pan?', he said, his almost green face nearly cracking under the strain of forced jocularity.

Barry had gone. It just showed you – you could do everything possible, try all you could, and something just stepped in and made all your efforts seem pathetic. Or humiliating.

At the end of the hangar Mason stopped and lit a cigarette, and stood there trying to decide whether to turn left and keep to the pathway, or go the long way round across the waste ground.

He'd go the long way, it was only 8.30. It was certainly keeping light these days. Then he remembered that tomorrow would be the longest day. That meant the shortest night. Not that there would be any appreciable difference between tonight and tomorrow night. There would be about four and a half hours of darkness up there. The trip should take six and a half to seven hours. That meant two and a half to three hours of daylight to contend with. The North Sea crossing would have to be done in daylight, and they should reach the Dutch coast about 11.30 or so. It wouldn't be really dark by then, not with a moon and this sky.

It was funny how the take-off times got later and later as the weeks went by and you didn't realise it until a night like this, when take-off time couldn't be any later. Then it got earlier and earlier until there was a margin of darkness to play with.

What a difference between tonight and the night of the crash, for instance. Take-off had been just after 4.00 that day and it was pitch dark, even without the snowstorm.

'It'll clear before you get back', the Met. Officer had said.

It was the last trip with Mason's original crew.

The take-off itself had been a nightmare, let alone the events that followed. The snow was falling so heavily it was only possible to see from one flare-path light to the other, and no way of knowing whether each one that came into sight was the end of the runway or not. Fifty feet up, the airfield was blotted out – too bad if you had a failure and wanted to get down again.

Mason didn't like that ice piling up on the leading edges either, and was anxious to get above the snow before it became too much for the de-icers to cope with. They broke through the cloud top into cold clear air, the stars mostly hidden from them by more clouds higher up. It was dark, beautifully dark.

The first thing to go wrong was the radio, half an hour after take-off.

Long said, 'Hello, captain. Wireless op here.' (Long always worked by the book.)

'Yes?'

'The set's u/s. Can't get a squeak out of it.'

Oh, hell.

'Definitely u/s? You've done all you can?'

'Everything. It was all right this afternoon, too.'

Well, that was that. If only they had found the fault before take-off. They'd have to go on without it. No excuse really to turn back now. The radio wasn't essential, not vital, but Mason hated things to be wrong. Things that had been put there for a purpose and not as an ornament. It was one chance less.

'All right', he told Long, 'but keep working on it.'

It was no use blaming Long, he was normally very conscientious, but Mason couldn't help feeling irritated. Mainly because he couldn't stop thinking about the useless radio.

About fifteen minutes later, though, he had something else to think about. At first it was just a sensation that something wasn't quite right. It was almost like the feeling of having left something behind, and Mason put it down to the fact that the radio incident had put him slightly off-datum, as it were. A little later he realised what it was and hurriedly scanned the instrument panel. The starboard engine was running a bit rough. There was no indication on the instruments but he could feel it, and he kept his eye on the dials, hoping against hope that it was imagination. Was the oil pressure needle dropping or wasn't it? He compared it with the port engine gauge, and tried to persuade himself it was the way he was sitting. Five minutes later there was no doubt about it and he cursed himself for pretending there had been. The pressure was obviously dropping, any fool could see that. There was no question of turning back yet – these things had a habit of righting themselves – much as he would have liked to.

He nudged Wood and pointed to the gauge. Wood leant over and peered at it, and by comparing it with the other dial, realised the trouble. He tapped it hopefully with his finger, then sat back with a shrug.

Far from righting itself the pressure dropped even more, then the engine revs began to fall. That was enough. There was no option. It would be madness to go on. 'We're turning back', Mason told the crew. 'An engine's gone sour.'

He asked Wood, 'The weather should have cleared by now, shouldn't it?'

Wood looked at the clock. 'Just about. By the time we get there.' Wood only took a moment to work out and write down the new course, and held the pad out.

Mason set the compass and headed for base, nursing the faulty engine, which as time went on grew slowly worse.

Ten minutes from base they began to drop through the cloud and met the snow again. It had eased off a lot but still cut down visibility.

'How are we going to let them know it's us and that we want to land?' asked Wood, thinking of the radio.

Mason had thought of that, and was a little worried about it. The flare-path would be out and nobody would be expecting them back. That wouldn't be so bad, because all they had to do was to fly around until somebody realised they wanted to come in, but they had to find the aerodrome first. It all depended on Wood. If his calculations were right they should pass close enough to pick it out.

'They'll know all right, once we find the 'drome.'

At five hundred feet he realised they would have to come much lower to pick out the airfield, and continued losing height. It was safe enough in this area, the only high ground being the Pennines, away over on their left, parallel with them. Should be. At three hundred feet Wood said, 'We should be there now', peering out a trifle anxiously.

'Can't see a bloody thing yet.' That was Plover from the front turret. It was the first time he'd spoken, except to say, 'Oh, pity', when they turned back.

Unless they passed clean over the airfield they wouldn't be able to see it even from this height, and Mason dropped lower. If they were going to find the aerodrome, it should be there now – somewhere underneath them. According to the clock and Wood's reckoning.

'Daren't go any lower', Mason said to everybody in general. 'We're down to two hundred feet. Can anybody see anything at all?' Drake from the tail: 'I thought I saw the main road just then. Not sure, though.'

Mason knew the road Drake meant and hoped he was right. They were near. After a moment or two of silence Wood said quietly, soberly, 'I'm sorry. I think we must have passed it.'

'All right. We'll do a search.' Couldn't blame Wood – a degree or two out would be enough in this weather, and it would be a good navigator, and a lucky one, to get nearer than that.

Mason put the machine into a shallow turn to begin
the outer ring of the search area. The snow seemed to be
half rain now as it dashed itself against the windscreen
and got blown off. Looking down through the depth of
the snow and rain it was only possible to see the area
directly beneath them.

He left the searching to the others. They were too
low to take chances against things looming up ahead.
There wouldn't be much time to avoid anything with this
visibility, it was true, but more time than there would be
if he wasn't looking. Not that anything should loom up
ahead, not in this vicinity, but there were such things as
faulty compasses, and navigational bloomers.

Wood was kneeling on the floor, his face pressed to
the window, his arms round his head to keep out all
distracting light. Plover, Mason knew, would be lying on
the floor of the turret doing the same. Drake in the tail
would be scanning the outer areas in the hope of seeing
a light the others might have missed through looking
down. Long was the only one who could do nothing. It
must have been worst for him, just sitting there, waiting
for someone to get him down safely, feeling naturally
but unnecessarily guilty at not being able to get them
a bearing. It was half-way round the first circle that it
happened. There was no time to warn anybody. Within
a split second of seeing it, before Mason even realised
what it was, he yanked the stick back hard into his stomach. The ground came rushing up at them as the nose
lifted, and flashed by a few feet below. The nose still up

and the ground still below, the aircraft was almost on stalling point when the ground slipped away and disappeared. The high ground, whatever it was, had gone and Mason quickly pushed the stick forward to get air-speed. Before he had time to collect himself it was there again, the ground rushing at them. As he pulled the stick back he knew they wouldn't make it this time. The engines hadn't regained their power, the starboard engine hardly answered at all, and this hill was higher. The nose went up, but over it he saw the hill-top for a fraction of a second, and then it was on them. There was a grinding tearing noise, a great shower of sparks from the engine on his left, the aircraft bucked and slewed – sparks, smoke, noise, a mighty jolt and he was thrown forward, and everything went vague and distant.

What seemed like hours afterwards but turned out to be only minutes, things became clearer and Mason was aware of Long standing over him. Wood was climbing out of the well, holding his shoulder. After him Plover crawled into the well from the front turret, dragging a leg.

'Christ', Long said, 'we're all alive.'

'Where's Drake?'

'He's all right. He's just getting the first-aid kit.'

Thank God there was no fire. They still had the bombs on board. Very lucky there.

When they'd all recovered sufficiently, and Mason had gone outside to make sure that the engines weren't going to catch fire after all, they got into the fuselage to examine their personal injuries. The lights were still working. Plover came off worst: he had a nasty gash on his leg, and Long and Drake bound it for him. Wood had been thrown into the well and hurt his shoulder, but didn't think anything was broken. Drake had a cut over his eye. Mason a clout on the head, and a pain in his chest. Long came off best without a scratch – all that happened to him was that his Thermos flask fell on his head long after the aircraft had come to a stop.

When they had sorted themselves out, drunk all the surviving coffee, and discussed their position, there was nothing to do but settle down for the long wait until daylight. There was nothing they could do that night. The snow had turned to rain, a fine misty drizzle cutting visibility down to a few hundred yards, and they didn't know where they were, except that it was somewhere in the foothills of the Pennines. It was a cold wait, and the lights failed somewhere around midnight.

They started out at first light but it was nearly mid-day before they got to a farmhouse. The going was bad, soft and slushy, and a thin wet fog lay upon the moors. Plover could do little more than hop, and had to be half carried by two of them. Long supported Drake, who hadn't realised the night before that he'd bruised his ankle. Before starting they had discussed the question of somebody going ahead to send a rescue party back, but the fog made it too risky, particularly as they didn't know exactly where they were. As long as they kept going they knew they would eventually reach help, and even Plover's pace quickened when, at last, the shape of the farmhouse appeared through the mist. Soon after, they were drinking cups of hot tea, eating cold lamb and boiled potatoes, their outer clothes drying in front of the range, the farmer's wife bustling about amongst them while the farmer went somewhere to phone. It was like waking from a nightmare. Sometime in the afternoon an ambulance arrived and took them to hospital.

VII

Six months ago, almost to the day. That was the longest night of the year, and felt like it. Tomorrow would be the shortest.

Mason decided he wouldn't go any higher than eight thousand feet tonight. With a sky as light as it would be tonight it would be wise to keep the horizon as high as possible. Might even come lower but that depended on the flak. Keep the fighters above you. They would want him above the horizon, silhouetted against the sky with themselves against the dark ground, lower down. The fighters would rely on the fear of flak to keep the enemy high. It all depended on the flak. Eight thousand wasn't very high for Düsseldorf – pretty hot place. The whole of the Ruhr was. 'Happy Valley', they called it.

If he'd had anything to do with the raid planning, he'd say that tonight was not the night to raid the Ruhr. But perhaps there was some particular reason for it. The target was an oil refinery on the banks of the Rhine.

Mason wondered if there were many people who realised how heavy and effective the German defences were compared with this country's. The night when he went over London by accident on his way back had been an eye-opener. It was true some of the flak had been fairly

93

close, and one of the lights caught them for a moment, but it hadn't worried him. He remembered wondering vaguely if there was a raid on, but thought it more likely they had strayed into a practice area. It didn't once occur to him that they were being fired at. It had been a great surprise to hear the next day that they'd been caught in a London barrage. It was amusing to hear some of the fighter chaps speaking like that. The time, for instance, when Bill and the rest of the crowd were in The Unicorn and heard one of these night-fighter fellows give a talk on the wireless about how he had been caught in this famous 'London barrage'. They hadn't known whether to be amused or angry. No doubt the bloke had been quite sincere, but he obviously hadn't seen a real barrage. He'd finished off by saying he was not allowed, for security reasons, to tell what method he'd adopted to get himself away from the flak. A great howl had gone up then, jeers and laughter mixed, because they all knew what the method was – they used it every night – stick the nose down and go like the clappers. While they were all laughing, Bill just sat there, his eyes blazing, repeating the words 'Line-shooting bastard'.

That wireless talk became quite a joke on the squadron and had lasted a long time; but there didn't seem to be anybody left now who remembered it. None of that crowd in The Unicorn were left – Bailey and Ward posted, and Trewsom and the rest gone.

It was that sort of thing Mason didn't like; there was nobody he could say 'Do you remember?' to.

Funny things didn't seem to happen now, things that became squadron jokes, like the time that chap with a name something like Pinkleton fell asleep and dropped off his chair during a Security Officer's lecture. It made Mason want to laugh even now to remember this great hulk of a fellow grovelling about on the floor, his eyes popping with amazement. But there was nobody left now he could laugh with about it.

This chap Pinkleton or Bumblefoot, or whatever his name was, had been the first of the crowd to go. Nobody had been surprised, though; in fact it was difficult to understand how he ever got through his exams. None of them had known him well because he'd suddenly turned up as one of their party, the day they joined the squadron. Or did he arrive a few days later?

Damn shame, really – the man was just plain stupid and quite unfit to accept the responsibility of taking an aeroplane and four other people into the air, let alone on a raid. That was the awful part: there were four others, all probably high-class men in their particular jobs.

Mason reached the living quarters and looked at his watch. Nearly nine o'clock – one hour to go. Nothing to do now but go to the mess.

His route would take him past Ken's room. He hadn't been that way for a long time. The last time had been when Dwyer had offered to lend him a clean shirt, and had asked him to go along to his room with him to fetch it. When Mason got there he found it was Ken's room, and it had come as a peculiar kind of shock to realise that

someone else was living there. The room looked different too. There weren't the same things on the table, and
jackets and trousers were hanging in the wrong places.
Some things were the same, though: the broken window-
catch caused when Ken came back late one night without
a key, and high up on the wall there were still signs of
the rude but clever ditty written by Trewsom one night
when they had a party. But even so everything was quite
different. Mason couldn't lounge across the bed with his
head against the wall and his feet on a chair as he would
have done had Ken been there. It had been difficult to
realise then that Ken had actually gone, and would never
again be seen in that room. Not under any circumstances,
not even if the war suddenly finished. But it was still a
case of Dwyer being in Ken's room.

He remembered saying to Dwyer, 'A friend of mine
used to have this room'.

'Oh?' Dwyer answered, rummaging in a drawer.
'What happened to him?'

'The big chop.'

Dwyer laughed. 'What are you trying to do, scare me?'

'Well, you know what they say about dead men's
shoes.'

It had been a joke and they both laughed. Now Dwyer
had gone and there'd be somebody else in Ken's room.

A pathway took Mason along the side of the living
quarters, and wireless sounds were coming from most of
the rooms because the windows were open. Here and
there he saw fellows he knew. Some were reading, some

writing, others just moving about. He nodded to one or two who happened to glance up.

In the old days he would have known the occupants of most of the rooms well enough to have stopped and talked, or to have just walked in. He wouldn't have had to spend a couple of hours wondering how to kill time.

As he passed Pepper's room, and began thinking of Pepper, Mason felt an extra – and distinct – feeling of sadness. More than sadness, it was a sort of chilly tremor, rather like driving through a mist-filled dip on a warm night. Pepper had been such a nice fellow, so honest and pleasant, so genuine and well-mannered.

There it was again – good fellows, bad fellows, rich or poor, clever or dull, they all went.

Turning right at the end of the block, Mason made for the mess. He couldn't hear any music so the dance couldn't have started. This rather angered him. If they were going to have a dance, why the hell didn't they get on with it? What right anyway had these ground wallahs to organise a dance on a raid night? To make it worse they didn't start it early enough. Not early enough for people like him, people who were trying to kill time on what might be their last evening on earth. It might be their last dance, their last glimpse of gaiety.

By the time he got to the door of the mess his sudden anger had gone, and he thought how unreasonable he was being. Nobody could foretell a raid night – nobody on the station, anyway. If they waited to find out, there would never be a dance, or a cricket match, or a football match, or anything that needed organising. No, theirs was the correct way. Everything must carry on smoothly. Dances must be held, and cricket or football matches, tennis, swimming, squash – everything which tended to camouflage the real purpose of the station. Because an aircraft or two might not return from a raid was no reason why entertainment or sport should be banned, or even discouraged. If an aircraft did fail to return, or two, three, or the whole lot, it didn't mean the station was finished. It had to go on until the war finished. Replacements for the cricket or football teams would be found, if necessary. New people would wander into the dances, none of them knowing anything of those they'd replaced, nor of those who would replace them. The aircraft would be replaced too, very quietly, as though they had really been there all the time.

It was funny when he came to think of it – except for the time he and Barry had gone to fetch that new aircraft, Mason had never seen a replacement aircraft delivered, nor heard of one. Nobody spoke of a new or an old aircraft. They all seemed new to him. In fact they were new, always.

It was a bit thick, though, not starting the dance yet. Entering the mess, Mason hung up his cap and made for the bar. It was fairly crowded, and as usual there seemed to be more females than males. Everybody was standing around in small groups, drinking, chatting, laughing. He gathered by odd snatches of conversation and the mopping of a brow here and there that the dancing had actually started, but things hadn't properly warmed up. He could see into the dining-hall, which was used for the dancing, and the band, as usual at the far end, was preparing to strike up again.

Mason glanced round the groups as he wormed his way to the bar. Nobody asked him to have a drink, and although he didn't expect it, he was conscious of it. They probably assumed, if they thought of it at all, that he was making his way to his own particular party – not realising, of course, that none of his party was left.

When he reached the bar he had to wait, because the steward was talking to a group at the other end, and the man brought in to help him for the evening was doing something with a lot of crates. The steward caught Mason's eye and indicated with a look that he would be along as soon as possible. When the steward could politely break away he moved along the bar and leant forward, lowering his voice: 'I was hoping ops would be scrubbed tonight.' He was a good chap, a 1918 veteran, and was trying to show that he thought it a little unfair that things were so unevenly balanced tonight.

'No chance of a scrubbing in this weather, Jim. Beer, please.'

The steward leant a little closer, casting a look around. 'It would do some of these others good to take your place tonight.'

It was difficult to tell to whom the steward was refer-ring, the civilians or the ground staff, but that sort of conversation had to be discouraged. Mason always found it rather embarrassing. It was assuming too much.

Fortunately there was no time to answer because a mixed group came noisily to the bar, and the steward, with a 'see what I mean' look, overloaded with significance, moved along to serve them.

Looking from this group round at other groups, Mason noticed how gay and very much at ease everybody seemed to be. It was so stupid that he should feel like a stranger and they should look so much at home. He could tell them all a thing or two, about the mess, the station – about the war.

He took his drink and wandered over to a vacant chair against the far wall. It was six minutes past nine.

Mason wished Saville hadn't gone off this morning. It had been a pleasant surprise to find old Saville sitting in the mess last night. He had forgotten all about him, and in any case it had never occurred to him that Saville would be coming back to the station, even though it was only to get his clearance papers.

It was the first time Mason had heard the full story of Ken's crash, of how Saville and Ken had somehow got out of the wreckage just before the main tanks blew up; of the young fitter who had been badly burned about the hands and arms trying to beat out Ken's blazing Irving jacket. 'Ken Minty was delirious all the time in hospital', Saville said. 'We were in the same room and he kept shouting and waking me up. He kept mentioning you – as though he was talking to you.'

'Oh, what sort of things did he say?'

'You know, silly things, like offering you a cigarette. Then once', Saville smiled slightly at the recollection, 'he called your name, a couple of times as though you hadn't heard the first time, and said something about "passing him a book", then he roared with laughter.' There was no point in telling Saville the long story about *Fatal Friday*, but it was pretty certain that was the incident in Ken's mind.

Saville hadn't been expected to live either, but though limping and scarred, there he was. It was a pity he only spent one night on the station, but after all those months in hospital it was only natural he should want to get cleared up and off home for his sick-leave as soon as possible. He must have gone very early this morning because he wasn't there at the normal breakfast time.

Saville was one of the lucky ones. He wouldn't be allowed to fly again, and would be given a ground job somewhere. He'd get through the war now, having done what he could to the best of his ability, and for the rest of his life his conscience would be clear, his pride intact. The point really being, he'd be alive to know. That was the great thing – to be alive at the end of the war with a conscience that was clear and open to inspection and criticism. It had nothing to do with patriotism. It is doubtful if anybody is ever willing to die for his country, or its king, its people, its mountains or its fields, its valleys or its beaches, its industries or its politicians. But many people would be willing to risk dying for the sake of their pride and their conscience. It might be just a question of what the neighbours would say. Was there any difference between pride and conscience, and what other people would say? Mason wondered.

The band was playing now, and couples began wandering off to dance, smiling, chatting and squeezing their partners' arms as they went. It was just like any other social gathering. If any of them were worrying about anything it was only the thought of getting up in the morning. If they were late for work or duty, as the case may be, their boss or commanding officer might become unpleasant. That was all. What a little thing to worry about. Mason knew the feeling – he used to get it. Not now, though. People in authority being unpleasant didn't worry him any more. It was a pity he couldn't tell all these people they had nothing really to worry about – their lives were protected by law.

Mason got up and walked towards the Gents and knew that from now until they took off he would have to keep on going. He used to get the same feeling at school, standing outside the Head's study waiting for punishment. Didn't know whether it was fear or excitement. He remembered asking one of the masters about it once, one he liked, Mr Chappell, the geography master.

Mr Chappell had looked down at him from his great height and roared with laughter. Still laughing, he had boomed, 'I don't know the exact cause of it, Mason, but unless your behaviour and work improve next term, you will have to have a special one all to yourself'. He and Roger had thought this the greatest of all jokes, and giggled throughout the day until caught by Mr Roughborough during maths, and were sent to the Head.

The door of the Gents swung open and somebody came in. Looking round, Mason saw it was Temple.

'Hello', said Temple. 'Damn shame having to leave this dance, isn't it?'

'Yes. Quite a crowd here tonight.'

There was nothing left to say, somehow, but Temple didn't seem to mind. He just stood there whistling, and Mason left him standing there.

Back at the bar it was easier to get a drink. Just one more and that would be the lot. He didn't really want that. Nobody had warned them about drinking before an op, but it seemed so natural not to, although before he had ever done an op he always thought that a couple of quick whiskies before take-off would be a good thing. But when it came to it, it was the last thing he thought of. Even the heaviest mess drinkers seemed to be affected the same way. There was only one chap Mason knew who had got into trouble for being drunk on an op night, and he, poor fellow, wasn't really to blame, because he thought ops had been scrubbed. It was an accident. All the same, they'd demoted him for six months, which meant he was off flying for that time. It was a very good party they gave him the evening of the day he was court-martialled. Simpson lost his cap again and somebody else broke a finger.

The dance was in full swing now, although there were

still people arriving. Mason thought he could do with something to eat. There should be some snacks around somewhere. He strolled through the dance hall into the kitchen, but was told by a couple of waiters he found in there, that they were very sorry, but the Mess President had given orders that no food was to be served until they got the say-so. It would probably be sometime after ten, they told him helpfully.

'Thanks', he said, moving off. Sort of thing the Mess President would do, the old bastard.

Mason stood watching the dancing and smoked. There was a girl in green he had noticed when she came in, and he looked for her. She had nice hair, not too wavy, and short. Then he saw her, not far from him, dancing with the Transport Flight Sergeant; she would come past him if they kept on the same course. She had really nice hair. Nice skin too, and carried herself well.

As they swung past him she was turned so that they came almost face to face. It could only have been for a split second, and he didn't know which had averted their eyes first, but in that moment Mason felt he had learnt far more about her than was possible by watching her from a distance for a whole evening. Her eyes were tender, but gay, and had a depth of affection that was almost breathtaking. He took a sly look in the direction in which they had gone but they had now spun away to the far corner and her back was to him.

What was the use, anyway? He'd have to go off soon, and in any case she was with somebody. Probably never

see her again. And even if he did, how could he compete
with blokes who only had normal worries to cope with,
and could behave naturally, planning ahead?

All the same, Mason was thinking as he walked off
the dance floor, he wished she was with him instead
of with that Flight Sergeant. Then he began to think
of Alice, and wondered what had happened to her. It
would be rather nice if she walked in now. It was a pity
that affair had to break up like that, so suddenly. She
was a nice girl and he liked her a lot. It could easily
have developed. Bill Bailey was partly to blame for that
break-up.

Thinking it over, though, that evening had had its
amusing points. It was just a pity he'd overlooked his date
with Alice. It had been on Mason's mind as they walked
into The Barley Mow and he'd mentioned it to Bill.

'Oh, plenty of time', Bill had said. 'We'll get there
in about twenty minutes on the old bike.' He jerked
his thumb towards his frail-looking motorbike leaning
against a wall, a pool of hot oil already forming underneath it.

They had needed a drink after that lecture. The 'old
man' had been at his most garrulous and had prattled on
for hours. 'Got verbal diarrhoea', Bill had muttered at
one point. The old man had a habit of dragging an entire
squadron of aircrews over to headquarters every so often
for these lectures.

Bill's idea had been all right to start with – that they
should do the twelve-mile journey on his motorbike

instead of going with the rest in the squadron bus. 'We can stop off at The Barley Mow for a couple on the way back', Bill had said, and that clinched the matter. But unfortunately that couple had led to others, and because they had got into one of their arguments – something very deep, like religion or politics – time had flown, and it was five past eight when they next looked at the time. Mason had arranged to pick up Alice at eight, twenty minutes' journey away.

Rushing to a phone, realising his voice was thick, he blurted, 'Sorry. Forgot, coming right away.'

She'd said something about there being no need to bother if he had something more interesting to do, and he said something even sillier, and after a few more angry remarks on both sides, she'd hung up.

Back at the bar he told Bill, and Bill had got just as angry.

'Old bit of junk, did she say?' he shouted. 'Perhaps it is, but it could do that journey in twenty minutes, easily.' There was fury in his slightly glazed eyes.

'Quarter of n'hour, Bill, if necessary.'

'Yes. Quar-ter nour', Bill blazed.

'Ten minutes', said a voice, and when they looked round there was a bumptious little man they hadn't noticed before, leaning against a corner of the bar, smirking round at the other people in the room, his gaze finally resting on Bill. Bill sent him a look like a flamethrower and the little man withered, and they forgot him. They then agreed hotly on the lack of reason in a woman's mental make-up and decided that a girl who nagged a chap just because he had a few beers wasn't worth bothering about, and settled down for the evening.

He'd never seen Alice again, although next day he wanted to phone but something happened and he couldn't, and the same the next day. Then when he did phone she was frosty because he hadn't phoned before, and it started all over again. After that came more ops, and the crash, and the whole thing petered out. What people like Alice didn't realise was that things moved so quickly these days.

Back at the bar, Mason looked at his watch. It was 9.20, and he wanted to go to the Gents again.

There were some civilians in there, and judging by their high spirits they were enjoying the dance. It made him think of the injustice one came across in wartime. The airmen who would have to sit around until the aircraft returned in the early hours of the morning weren't allowed in the officers' mess, dance or no dance, but these civilians were. When they in turn joined up they would be barred themselves. It was obviously unjust, but nobody had been able to think of a solution. Unless it was 'Don't join up without a rank of some sort'.

Coming out of there, Mason stood for a moment in the bar being jostled by the crowd coming off the dance floor, a little uncertain where to go now. In an attempt to move out of the crowded area his shoulder came into contact with somebody and he turned to apologise – and for the second time that evening came face to face with the girl in green. Looking into those eyes he felt the same momentary breathtaking sensation.

'I'm sorry', he said.

She was smiling now, a nice friendly smile. 'It was my fault', she answered, 'for standing right in the way.'

He looked round instinctively for the Flight Sergeant but couldn't see him. 'Didn't I see you with our Transport King?'

She laughed easily, mouth slightly open, and her eyes twinkled as she laughed. 'Is that what you call him? He's over in that crowd getting drinks.'

Having actually met her, Mason didn't want to leave her before it was necessary. He felt not the slightest trace of shyness towards her, and she seemed so natural and at ease. 'Why don't you wait over there where it's less crowded? He'll find you more easily there anyway.'

She glanced over her shoulder. 'Yes, I think I will.' She turned with a smile that in no way dismissed him and he followed her, noticing the smooth lightness of her walk as she threaded her way towards some armchairs pushed up against the far wall. Reaching them, she didn't sit but turned to him, apparently not worried or annoyed by his presence.

'Yes, he'll find you here all right', Mason said, more for something to say.

'He won't worry a great deal if he doesn't. In fact, I'm probably being a nuisance to him.'

She wasn't being serious, of course, and he looked at her to make sure.

'He's the husband of a friend of mine', she explained, 'an old school friend, and I'm staying with them. They couldn't both come because of the baby. I offered to stay but my friend insisted that I came.'

The Flight Sergeant came over to them with her drink. 'Sorry to be so long', he said. Then realising she wasn't alone, went on, 'Do you mind if I leave you for a bit? Just met a fellow I haven't seen since we first joined. He's only visiting.' The Flight Sergeant turned to Mason with a grin and said, 'Do you mind looking after her for a while?'

'Not at all. But I'll have to go soon.'

'Thanks.' The Flight Sergeant turned back to the girl. 'I won't be long anyway.'

When he had gone there was a moment's silence before the girl spoke. 'How soon will you have to go?' Was there a note of disappointment in her voice? Well, there probably was, because she would be left alone. Mason looked at his watch. 9.30. 'In about fifteen minutes.'

'Rather late to go anywhere, isn't it? Or shouldn't I pry?'

He returned her smile. 'No, it's not too late – not where I'm going. And you shouldn't pry.'

A slight look of distaste came to her face at the turn the conversation had taken, and he hastened to correct the impression he must have given. She obviously didn't realise there were ops on tonight.

'Not what you're thinking. I'm working. Won't you sit down?'

'Oh, sorry', she laughed, sinking into a chair. 'I didn't think of that. Are you on night duty then?'

'Yes, yes I am.'

She noticed he hadn't got a drink. 'Is that why you're not drinking?'

'Mm.'

'I thought there must be some reason. I've always understood that aircrew fellows …' She broke off, hesitated a moment before turning fully to him, her eyes on his face, then down to the wings above his breast pocket, and back to his face again. He felt embarrassed before her gaze and turned away. 'So that's where you're going', she said.

'How stupid of me', she went on, quietly, looking round the room. There was a moment of silence before she turned to him again, smiling. 'You know', she said, 'you're the first bomber pilot I've met. Oh, I've read about them in the papers, of course, but somehow you never think of people you read about as being real until you meet them.'

He still felt slightly embarrassed and couldn't think of an answer.

'How often do you go on these raids?' She was showing a new interest now and somehow Mason didn't mind talking to her about it.

'It depends mainly on the weather. In good weather we might go three or four nights running, then we might go weeks doing nothing except routine flights over this country. Tonight will be the third night running.'

He was actually enjoying talking to her about it. She said nothing for a moment while she looked around at the people in the room. Then she said, 'What time will you get back tonight?'

That was an awkward question, and Mason had said too much already really. He glanced automatically at the slogans – 'Be like Dad, keep Mum' – which here and there adorned the walls, and shifted a little uncomfortably before answering. 'I don't want to sound melodramatic or mysterious but we're not supposed to talk about operations.'

To his relief she didn't laugh or do anything to suggest that he was being over-conscientious or making a drama out of nothing.

'Of course.' She was quite serious. 'Silly of me. I'm sorry.'

The conversation became easy again after that. She told him she lived in London, and that she was waiting to hear the result of her application to join the WAAF. One subject led into another easily and naturally, and all the while the hands of Mason's watch moved nearer to the time when he would have to go. At a quarter to ten he said, 'I'm afraid I must go now', and watched to see what effect this would have on her. The result caused a thrill of pleasure to run through him, as she turned to him, frankly disappointed. She smiled slightly as she said, with that openness that he liked so much, 'I'm sorry you've got to go'.

Mason got up and stood a little awkwardly in front

of her, reluctant to go. It was on the point of his tongue to ask if he could meet her again, but something stopped him. It was nothing to do with her manner – he was sure she would agree. But it was planning ahead, tempting fate, a thing he never did these days. Suddenly, he had become sad and depressed.

'Goodbye', she said. 'Perhaps we will meet again some day, when I'm in the Air Force.'

He had taken a step back and was half turned to move off when that remark stopped him. As she looked at him her expression caused in him a wild, foolish desire to go to her and bury his face in her lap and tell her he didn't want to go tonight. She would understand.

'Good night', he smiled at her and turning on his heel walked quickly towards the door. On the way he decided he wouldn't look round at her again, but at the door, on an impulse, he turned. She was looking in his direction and at first her expression was serious. Then she smiled and waved a hand, and with that smile Mason felt the same surge of happiness and pleasure that she had aroused before, except that now there was a certain relief mixed up somewhere in his emotions. At first he couldn't identify the sensation, although he knew it was not entirely unfamiliar, but suddenly he remembered. It was like catching a glimpse of sun and blue sky while climbing through black thunderclouds, or the first sight of the ground when descending through fog.

He waved his hand in return and went through the door onto the porch. The sun was sinking behind the skyline of the station buildings, a small part of the great red ball still visible, and he stood on the top step watching it until it had disappeared.

'This is what is known as a lovely evening', Mason thought to himself as he descended the steps and walked slowly towards the hangars. He didn't even know her name. And that's how it should be.

VIII

It was pretty early to start getting ready but that was better than a last-minute panic. Anyway, what was the time now? He might as well have got togged up this morning and hung around the crew-room all day in his flying kit. It would have been boring, that was all. He'd gained nothing by walking about all day, in and out of the mess, to his room and back, all for no reason. The walk to the village had been profitable, but twenty cigarettes – although very acceptable – had only a sort of local importance. They added nothing to his life. Time-killing without them would have been a little harder, that's all there was to it. Like those two beers he'd had, like having the mess to go to, the band to listen to, the dancers to look at, the girl in green to talk to – they were all things to make the process of time-killing appear to be less of a waste of time.

Was that why anybody did anything? Was the whole of one's life made up of time-killing incidents? Obviously some people had found better ways of doing it than others, war or no war. Those who were rich could do it at a higher standard than those who weren't. Others might have achieved something. But for the vast major-ity, who had neither the money nor the satisfaction of

115

achievement, life could become, and in lots of cases must have become, an exceedingly tedious string of trivial, incidental events. Some might say they had had a fine game of tennis or had watched a good football match. Would they have had a more enjoyable time than the person who had slept the entire afternoon? The answer, of course, was that they had found a way of killing an afternoon successfully. And if life is like that, why do people fear death so much, when in death the whole problem would be automatically solved?

What, then, was he afraid of? Mason knew he was frightened of the pain he would experience – even if you're killed 'instantly', as they say, you must feel something before you actually die – but he wasn't sure if that was all he was afraid of. He'd experienced pain before and knew it wasn't the pain that killed you but the thing which caused the pain.

No, it couldn't be the fear of pain. Then it must be the fear of being dead, and not of dying. And yet, life was merely a struggle to amuse and entertain yourself until you died of old age. One surely didn't cling to life for that reason – just so as to die of old age?

Probably everybody clung desperately to life for as long as possible because they feared the unknown. When they killed time for themselves they knew what was happening, but to have the necessity of killing time taken away – to have time killed for them in an unknown manner – was a different thing, and as such, was frightening.

It was, then, without a doubt, being dead that Mason was afraid of.

Anyway, whichever way he looked at it, he was back where he started – still frightened.

It was rather a surprise on reaching the crew-room to find somebody already there. It was Lane, a navigator, and he had evidently just finished making some last-minute adjustments to his maps and notes. He was putting them away into a carrier and looked up as the door opened.

'Hello', Lane said. 'You're early. Keen type, eh?'

'Early, yes. Keen type, no.'

Mason watched Lane finish packing his navigation paraphernalia and was glad he wasn't a navigator, having to lug all that stuff around: maps, notes, code-charts, instruments. Identification signals to worry about – all fiddling things.

'I hear you're being posted', Lane said suddenly.

'Yes, in about a week.'

'Your rest period, of course? Do you know where you're going yet?'

'Scotland. Ops training – unless I go for a burton before.' He didn't know why he said that to Lane and smiled to show he wasn't really worried about it.

Lane smiled too but became serious again and said, 'What do you honestly think our chances are of getting through – even our first tour?'

'Well' – Mason had slung off his respirator and was unbuttoning his tunic – 'I've never tried to work out the actual percentages. And you'll never see them printed anywhere.' That bottom button was coming off. Must get it done.

'I've done fifteen now', Lane was saying, 'and when I think I'm only half-way through, I can't see much chance of getting away with it for another fifteen times, without the extra couple they seem to chuck in for luck these days.'

Mason didn't know Lane thought that way, and felt a sudden liking for him. He wanted to cheer him up by saying he'd got through 30, but wasn't that rather asking for it? That business again of tempting fate, or something? He hadn't finished his tour yet. There was tonight, and probably at least another trip after that, if he wasn't being posted for a week. There was the case of Barclay the other night, missing on his 32nd op – the last of his tour. Lane broke in again, just as Mason was trying to think of something to say.

'Tough luck on old Ted Barclay, wasn't it?'

Mason looked quickly at Lane but he was busy taking off his tunic and gave no appearance of having knowingly read his thoughts.

'Damn tough.' He began taking off his collar and tie. 'Not much hope either.'

'Why?' Lane was taking his tie off. 'Have you heard anything?'

'The Signals Section say they picked up the aircraft asking for a bearing, but it seemed as though the aircraft wasn't receiving anything. Then they went out of range and that was the last heard of them. Must have passed clean over England and come down in the drink.'

Both had their tunics, collars and ties off now.

'Poor devils', Lane said as they began to walk across the corridor into the locker-room, and his far-away look was obviously a reflection of the picture he had in his mind of the scene in the aircraft that night: anxious eyes peering out into the darkness, looking for a break in the clouds, hoping for it to coincide with something they could identify their position by, a beacon, a lake, a river – anything. And all the while the engines would be droning on, relentlessly, taking them they knew further and further away from their last known position, which might have been as far back as the enemy coastline. The atmosphere would be tense, with long periods of silence, words passed only when necessary, and then in the shortest possible sentences, clarity being far more important than grammar – the radio operator feverishly working on his morse-key, probably unaware that his receiver was faulty.

'Lot of cloud that night', Lane went on as they reached the locker-room. 'Wind changed too, if I remember.'

There were a couple of other chaps already in there, and after a minute or two the rest began to drift in. The room filled with noise: locker doors slamming, laughter, swearing, and chatter – that bright, brittle chatter of voices pitched a little higher than normal, laughter a little too gay, in some cases sounding harsh and unreal because it required more effort than usual. Everybody was very happy-go-lucky, and oh, in such high spirits.

Looking down the room, Mason saw Lane at the far end, and noticed that he was taking no part in this back-chatting gaiety while he quietly pulled on his parachute harness. He had often spoken to Lane, at meals, in the bar and so on, but he didn't realise that he had got over his 'I'll get through if nobody else does' phase. He felt sorry for him, as he did for everybody who began to develop those nagging doubts.

Mason pulled on his second boot, took his helmet, intercom and gloves out of the locker, shut the door and went back to the crew-room.

'Hello, Les', a voice said behind him, loudly. It was Harper, of course. He was the sort of bloke who wouldn't realise how he hated being called 'Les'.

'All ready?'

Harper shouted back, 'Will be in a jiffy', and disappeared into the locker-room.

Why did some people irritate others? And why were some people irritated by others? One was often inclined to think that because you, personally, found a particular person irritating, that person must be an irritating person. That couldn't be so, or otherwise that fellow Harper, for instance, would have no friends at all. So his friends must be irritating too, working on the birds of a feather principle. That meant you had two main groups, both groups thinking the other irritating. Amusing thought, that.

Mason wondered how many people found him irritating, and suddenly, with quite a shock, he realised that these days he had no real friends on the station. So presumably they all found his company unattractive. Horrible, really. The fact that he didn't try to make friends made no difference – they weren't to know he hadn't always been like that. Others had probably tried to be friendly with him but he hadn't reciprocated, and was therefore considered morose or bad-tempered, or supercilious, or just plain unfriendly. Or irritating. A pity that, but he couldn't help it. Hell, what did it matter anyway? His friends were in his memory, and he still gained comfort from their company. And there was Bill Bailey – good old understanding Bill.

Somebody came into the crew-room carrying a bag of rations and a Thermos of coffee. Better go and get his.

When he got back the crew-room was full, and very noisy. The fellows were standing about in groups, mostly in crews, and he looked for his crew. Tomlinson was there, talking to Holt, and as he joined them Dent walked up. Only Harper to come now. Over in the corner Lane was standing a little apart from his crew, gazing at a wall poster which he must have known by heart because it had been there as long as Mason could remember.

The C.O. came into the room in tennis clothes but wearing his uniform cap, jumped onto the table and shouted above the din that the tenders were outside waiting.

The fellows began filing through the door and Mason walked out with Tomlinson and Holt, Dent following. The C.O. was now standing just inside the door and as they passed he nodded, grinning, and said, 'Good trip, Mason'.

He nodded back. 'Thank you, sir.' It worried him rather that the C.O. should have said that. He hadn't said it to anybody else. Was it anything to do with these last two trips, so near and yet so far? Nice of him but rather disturbing.

'Where's Harper?' Dent said from behind Mason.

'Christ knows. Give him a yell, will you?'

Dent put his head into the locker-room and almost collided with Harper as he came blundering out.

They all managed to get into the same tender. It was very noisy and crowded, full of flying kit, boots, parachute packs and navigators' bags. It was hot too. Then everybody started shouting to the driver as though he was the one holding things up. 'Contact!' 'Pull the chocks away!' 'Time to get up, driver!' 'Pull your finger out!' '"B for Bunty" first!' 'Hurry up, I feel bloodthirsty!' Somebody started singing, taken up by several others, 'They scraped him off the tarmac like a pound of strawberry jam'. To a crescendo of shouting, singing and cheering they started off, and somebody who had chosen that moment to stand up fell onto everybody else, and then rolled to the floor, where in spite of his shouts he was prevented from getting up, adding something extra to the noise and confusion.

It was more comfortable when one crew got out at the first aircraft.

Mason was glad 'G for George' was the last machine – it meant they would be longer in the tender. He realised how stupid that would sound if he told anybody, but it was quite true, he did feel like that. It was putting things off just that little bit longer. He wondered if the tender could go on and on until the end of the war. When they got to 'G for George' and had to get out he felt a strange reluctance to do so. It frightened him a little, to feel like that. It had never happened before, about getting out of the tender. When he jumped down it was like breaking another thread.

The van turned round and Mason stood and watched until it disappeared behind a gun emplacement, knowing while he did so that it must have seemed odd to the ground crew, if any of them were watching. The rest of his crew wouldn't notice; they were getting into the aircraft.

It was a peculiar feeling, watching that tender going away, leaving them out there with the aircraft. It seemed as though another link had been broken. That link would only be reconnected after they had taken off, gone to the Ruhr and back, and landed again. It was such a small link to support that great weight.

Mason turned and walked to the machine, and one of the ground crew held the steps while he climbed in. That damned smell. Why did aircraft have to have that smell? Sweet, sickly and, well – yes, it was a deathlike smell. 'Smell of death' – that was more like it, because it suggested the future, whereas 'deathlike smell' suggested something past. Ken had mentioned something similar once; so had Bill Bailey.

As he slid into his seat Mason became aware of the other aircraft engines starting and warming up. The clock on the instrument panel said 10.25. Better get cracking. Over on the left 'S for Sugar' seemed all ready to move off to the runway. The steps had been taken away, and one of the ground crew was waving, probably answering the pilot's thumbs-up signal.

Mason's eye caught a movement on the ground beneath him and he realised a mechanic was trying to attract his attention, wanting to know if he was ready to start the engines. He gave thumbs-up and glanced round the cabin to see if the others were ready. They were all absorbed in their own jobs and apparently had no trouble to report.

One engine started up straight away with a great roar. Mason could never understand why those flames that shot out didn't set fire to the whole machine. The terrific rush of air from the airscrew, of course, kept them in one direction and away from the fuselage, but even so, they seemed awfully close.

What the hell was wrong with the other engine? The damned thing started all right this afternoon. They tried again but it showed no signs of firing. One of the mechanics shouted to him, and climbing on top of the engine, took the cowling off and began fiddling about with something inside.

They tried again. Still no good, and the mechanic climbed up again. Another one stood on the top of the steps helping him. Might as well switch the other engine off. 'S for Sugar' began to move off. They were supposed to follow her.

There was a roar from the far end of the runway. That was the first machine taking off, and they hadn't warmed up yet. 'B for Bunty' passed very close on the left, only a few feet up, with that crackling roar of engines at full boost, as though they were angry. One of the crew stuck two fingers up at Mason. Mechanically he stuck two up in answer.

And still that bloody engine wouldn't start. The Flight Sergeant Mechanic had come over and taken charge. Then the C.O. arrived to see what the trouble was.

Another machine went off: 'M for Mother'. That was Lane's aircraft – hope he'd be all right.

They seemed to have half the engine spread all over the aerodrome now. 'G for George' might not be able to go tonight, and there was no spare machine. If those blokes down there knew what Mason was thinking they would probably call him unpatriotic, or a coward or something.

He looked round as he heard the next machine approaching. It passed almost overhead but he managed to read 'C' on the side. 'C for Charlie' – that was Simpson. Might have known it: it was a miracle how he always managed to get his aircraft into the air without having to use all the runway. Good luck, cock, you've got a date tomorrow.

Better get out and show a little interest. Keen, annoyed at this delay, that's what he must be. But just as Mason was getting out of his seat the Flight Sergeant looked up at him with a proud smile and gave thumbs-up, confident that he'd cured the trouble, very pleased with himself. The rest of the ground crew began putting the parts back into the engine, anxious to get it done as soon as possible. As Mason sat back another aircraft went over. One more to go besides him.

It was hot sitting there – the machine had been in the sun all day. It was like a greenhouse, and they were being ripened. Mason recognised Dent's voice over the intercom asking the time. Twenty to eleven, Holt told him. Tomlinson said he was hungry and was going to start on his rations.

They were putting the cowling back. The Flight Sergeant watched them impatiently until the last screw was put into place, and then turned and waved a hand, indicating that they were ready. 'S for Sugar' roared past, and everything became quiet. The Flight Sergeant was wiping his hands on a bit of rag as though he didn't expect to have to dirty them again. The first engine started again without any trouble, and Mason flipped the switch for the other engine, conscious that all eyes below were gazing expectantly. He pressed the button and the blades began slowly to turn. Suddenly a puff of blue smoke and the engine burst into life with a shattering triumphant roar. Everybody on the ground was all smiles and looking up at him. They'd done a good job.

Mason pretended to be concentrating on the instrument panel – it was easier. The C.O. got into his car, waved and drove off.

Mason ran the engines up in the routine manner, concentrating a little more on the one which had given the trouble. Revs all right, pressure all right – they were both running beautifully. The fellows on the runway must be wondering what had happened. A final searching look along the instrument panel, and he gave the okay. Two fellows pulled the blocks away, and as he started to taxi, the ground crew waved. He and the others in the cabin waved back. One of the ground crew chaps stood watching as the others started walking towards the dispersal unit. Mason waved a hand and the chap answered, before passing out of sight behind the machine.

The ground was very bumpy – perhaps he was going too fast. Mustn't forget that dip where Pepper tipped his aircraft over onto a wing and wrecked an undercarriage. Mustn't do that tonight. It would be quite easy: just a little too fast, one wheel in the dip, and that would be that. Mason knew exactly where it was and left it a long way over on his right. He turned the machine towards the head of the runway.

They were waiting for him, of course, when he arrived. He swung the aircraft round onto the runway and allowed her to come to a stop, the engines ticking over. The Duty Officer was giving him the all-clear. They were late, nearly five to eleven. Mason switched on the intercom. 'Here we go, chaps.'

IX

The engines roared up and the machine began to move. Thank heavens for the Double Summer Time, and that it was still light. Mason hated taking off at night, tearing along in the dark and rising into nothing, with all sense of direction and balance gone, relying on a few man-made instruments. Much better being able to see for yourself the ground slipping past underneath, faster and faster, the hedge getting nearer, and watching the corner of the sick quarters because you knew when you got level with it the aircraft should be ready to lift. And then when the aircraft became buoyant as the wheels left the rough ground, watching the ground appear to be slowing down as the machine rose, a dispersal hut passed underneath, then the hedge and rusty barbed wire, the road and fields, lots of fields and lots of hedges in squares and oblongs, small things moving about, cows, horses, cars, people.

They were high enough to turn now. Better not waste time doing circuits, he'd climb on track – rules or no rules. Didn't want to get to the target area too far behind the others and have no one to share the defences with. There might be one or two still there; it depended on how long they took to find the target. Doubtful, though. Nobody would want to hang around the Ruhr tonight for longer than was absolutely necessary. 'S for Sugar' might still be there. It was possible.

At a thousand feet he flattened out a little. The ground was rather hazy now. Down there it would be twilight but up here it was like early evening. How still everything seemed down there. Still and cosy, peaceful. He could make out a village here and there. There was nothing more peaceful, Mason thought, than a village from the air. That little place down there, for instance, with its village green and small pond. He hoped the green wasn't littered with broken bottles and rusty tins, and that the pond was kept clear of bits of old prams and tin baths. Distance was a thing which kept beauty and disillusionment apart.

The village seemed quite deserted. He supposed people in those houses and cottages would be taking a final look at the children in their cots before turning in themselves. Those already in bed and on the point of sleep might be turning over grumpily at the noise the aircraft were making. They'd probably heard the others go over and thought that was the lot, and so had settled down. Others, perhaps, would be thinking of them in a different way, thinking in terms of men in the aircraft – mere boys in some cases – and not of the aircraft themselves. Like the lady who had given Mason a four-leafed clover one day. It had happened in a crowded bus and he often wondered if he'd thanked her properly because he'd been rather embarrassed at the time. It was a pity he couldn't let her know he'd still got it and carried it always, not through superstition, but out of respect for her. Nobody else had ever seen it or knew of it. He couldn't stand that habit some blokes had of going around with rabbits' feet or lucky elephants, or something, lashed to their breast pocket button. They were usually the fellows who fixed ridiculous fluffy toys to the dashboard of their aircraft, or on their guns or radio apparatus.

Tomlinson was a little inclined to do that sort of thing – he had a tiny celluloid airman tied to his parachute pack. It was different with Tomlinson, somehow, because he wasn't really that type. He was a strong-minded, responsible chap with a misleading air of casualness. Good navigator too. He was always so calm – no, more than calm – unmoved, that's the word.

Mason turned his head and looked at Tomlinson now. Amazing fellow, just staring idly out at the ground, munching raisins. Didn't look as though he was even thinking. He didn't look as though he ever did any thinking, and yet when it came to a navigation problem he was quick, sharp and sure.

Damned good crew altogether, really. Except for Harper, perhaps, who strangely enough had been very quiet so far. Not liking it a bit, I bet, stuck out there in the front turret. Too bad, that's what he joined the Air Force for, and in any case, he would only have to do that until he'd done enough ops to become captain of an aircraft. Not like Dent, crammed into the rear turret, far away from everybody. That would be his job for as long as the war lasted – or he lasted. Just sitting there, hour after hour, without being able to stretch his arms or legs, never knowing what was really going on, particularly during those long periods of silence when things were really happening. Mason liked Dent, a cheery little chap with bags of energy. It must be harder for him than most to sit there doing nothing. He'd call him up.

'Hello, tail gunner. Everything all right?'

'Hello Leslie, yes, fine thanks. Just one point, though, is it going to get dark before we reach the Jerry coast?'

'Oh yes, more or less. The night fighters will have a little protection.'

Dent was chuckling as Tomlinson's voice came in: 'We should see Flamborough Head any moment now. Can you see anything, Harper?'

A few grunts came through the phones. Harper was obviously making hard work of it. 'I can see … oh, bugger this thing … I can see coastline, and I think that's the Head, a little to our right. Not sure yet, though.'

Tomlinson glanced down and stared for a while. Taking a look at the map on his knee he stared down again, and having satisfied himself, passed his pad over with the new course written down. The first stage was over. The North Sea now. Tomlinson settled back.

Dent's voice suddenly came through the phones.

'Aircraft on the starboard quarter – some distance off.'

Mason glanced round quickly.

'Can't see from here. Which way is it going?'

'Coming towards us. Fairly high up. He's seen us because I saw him turn. Too far away to identify.'

'We'll get down to sea level', Mason told everybody in general and pushed the stick forward, opening the throttles wider. He hoped his voice sounded normal. Tomlinson was peering round, half standing.

'He's coming in – started diving', Dent called excitedly. The intercom system crackled, little chattering crackles. Dent again: 'He's pulling out – wait a minute, I think it's a Spitfire – he's climbing – yes, it's a Spit. Sorry.' Thank God for that. 'All the same', Mason told Dent, 'if he does come in, don't let him open up first.' He found it hard to keep the relief out of his voice.

'Don't worry.' It was obvious Dent had no intention of letting the Spitfire do any such thing. Quite right too. There were too many of these trigger-happy Spitfire fellows flying around. That was how Cole got his lot, and there were others too.

Mason tried to think of the time he and Cole, with several other chaps, had spent a hilarious evening in a neighbouring village. He always tried to think of something like that when that fluttery feeling started. It usually worked but tonight he couldn't control his thoughts. When he concentrated on Cole and that village pub, the pictures wouldn't stay there. No matter how hard he tried. Forcing them back wasn't doing any good. Making him worse if anything. Making him frightened, because he couldn't do it. Shouldn't have thought of Cole. It was the association between Cole and that Spitfire that was doing it, stopping him from controlling his thoughts and so preventing that fluttery feeling. His knees were shaking. Couldn't remember that happening before. His hands too would shake if he didn't grip the control column hard. His heart was pumping and he was getting that awful feeling in his chest as though, inside, it was shivering. He hoped nobody would speak to him and want an answer. His jaw was tight, because he had to clench his back teeth to stop it shivering. Mustn't be a fool – it was only a Spitfire, and it had gone now anyway. Try to think of something else. What, though? This thing wouldn't let him think of anything else. You're working yourself up into a panic. What would he be like later when there was real danger? God, it was getting worse. He was breathing in jerks. Oh God.

He reached for his bag of rations. The chewing gum, get the chewing gum. He didn't usually start on it until much later. Must do something, though. Often, chewing gum had helped, but he had never had anything as bad as this. It was amazing what a difference it made – just chewing. The only person he had ever discussed it with had been Ken.

The chewing gum was the only thing Mason ever touched of his rations. It was funny how the speed of chewing varied in direct proportion to the degree of fear. Ken had found the same thing, and they used to laugh about it. Sometimes when a trip was worse than usual and they met in the Ops Room on their return, they would hold their aching jaws and roar with laughter.

A lot of thought must have gone into the selection of the rations. It had taken several trips for Mason to understand why the packets were made up of such widely varied and apparently mismatched articles. It wasn't their food value which mattered so much. Nobody was expected to scoff the lot. Nobody he knew would go from an orange to butterscotch, to raisins, to wine-gums, to chocolate, swill it all down with coffee and then chew the gum. There never seemed time to do all that. One was only expected to choose the thing or things which seemed to help. Mason could well imagine some other guy eating an orange because of his dry throat, like him with the chewing gum, at the same stage of each trip. Other fellows would find something else helped more. But everybody had to take a complete pack otherwise the whole psychological point would be lost. You couldn't line everybody up just before a trip and say, 'Hands up all those who feel calmer when they chew gum', and so on right through the list.

Slowly at first, then all of a sudden, Mason became aware that his knees were now steady. And the panic in his chest had gone. The relief made him feel almost gay. He wanted to laugh. He wanted to laugh loudly – roar with laughter, scream with laughter. It had worked, but it was nothing to do with chewing gum itself. He sniggered into his oxygen mask. It was only thinking about the gum, or the orange, or the raisins or the chocolate that did it. Merely something to alter your train of thought. Thinking that any one particular thing could do it was only the first stage. It was what that thing made you think about that really mattered.

So perhaps it hadn't been so difficult to select the ration items. But it was clever of somebody to realise that.

Mason eased himself back in his seat more comfortably and noticed Tomlinson glance round at the movement. It made him wonder if he'd given any signs of what he'd been going through. No, Tomlinson's manner was quite normal as he gazed out the window.

He wondered what Tomlinson was thinking about. What was in the minds of the rest of the crew, at this moment? Tomlinson, as usual, didn't look as though he was thinking of anything. He was leaning back in his seat, looking out at the darkening sky, one hand resting on the window catch, tapping a finger, probably humming. Actually, he was quite likely checking over in his mind the calculations he had made for the course home, after this bombing business was done with. He didn't look as though he needed anything out of the rations to calm him down.

One could never tell, though; maybe that was why Tomlinson had those raisins. Tonight he had started on them earlier, that was all. That talk about being hungry might have been an act – so he could start on the raisins without it seeming odd. His hunger may have been genuine, of course. Perhaps he always did get hungry on a trip – but for raisins.

In a way Tomlinson was a similar type to Holt. You could never really get to know either of them. Both were responsible without being serious.

Holt at the moment was probably reading. Most

wireless ops did that during the radio silence on the
way out, and it was quite safe for them to have the
panel light on, with the blind drawn across. It was hard
to imagine being able to read a book under the circumstances, but they seemed to find it possible. Mason
couldn't believe it was just boredom, though. Certainly
not in Holt's case.

Dent was different. He was a little more transparent.
Cheerful, good-natured and kind-hearted, thinking more
than likely not of himself but of his folks, or his girlfriend.
He had mentioned a brother in the Merchant Service.
Looking at the area below may have set his mind thinking of his brother's ship, ploughing through the Atlantic,
wondering if she was in the last convoy attacked; wondering if she'd been sunk, his brother drifting on a raft,
miles from anywhere; wondering if he was dead, floating
full of water, in a flooded cabin, engine-room or fo'c'sle.
Pretty awful having relatives to worry about as well.

And Harper – God knows what he was thinking
about. Probably regretting he'd ever signed on as aircrew. Or, better still, wishing he could wear the uniform
without having to fly on ops.

Was he perhaps being a little unfair to Harper? The
fellow was a coward – no doubt about that – but was
it entirely his fault? People couldn't always help being
cowards. It was just the way they were made. Anyway,
it was difficult to decide exactly what a coward was. He,
Mason, was afraid of ops. Hated them. No good saying,
'Ah, but you're not shirking ops', because neither was

Harper – there he was, in the front turret. Couldn't really blame anybody for not liking ops anyway: nobody did, though some got a kick out of the tension and excitement before, and the relief afterwards.

But with Harper it was different. He had obviously been attracted by the glamour, but now realised that the danger which he had treated so lightly, and hoped somehow would never come, was there, and very real. He had looked upon it as a thrill with an element of danger to add a touch of glamour. He had had the thrill, and would now willingly give up the glamour, if this was what he had to have with it, but it was too late. Like an actor's first-night flop, his first trip had shaken his complacency. So it might have been just a case of his conceit getting the better of his somewhat limited intelligence.

Oh, it was all very well trying to work things out like that, but Mason didn't like the idea of Harper being in the aircraft. Couldn't be trusted in an emergency – couldn't be trusted anyway.

Mason thought it would be interesting to know if any of the others were wondering what he was thinking. If it was possible to read each other's minds, they would know he was wondering what they were thinking, and he would know they were wondering what he was thinking. What a hell of a complicated thing, the mind. All sorts of things popping into it, never still for a moment. Darting from one place to another, from one thing to another. If anyone, now, asked him what he was thinking he wouldn't be able to tell them. Actually, right at the moment he was wondering what answer he would give if they asked him.

But that wasn't all Mason had in his mind. There was something else, right at the back, which was there all the time, whatever else he was thinking. Something well-planted, almost solid, like a slightly aching tooth, or a stone in your shoe. Whatever else he had in his mind, any time, anywhere, that thought would never be far away, always ready to pop forward at the least excuse. There were so many things which brought it to the front, again and again. More often than not, only fleetingly, just to make sure it wasn't forgotten. Things like the words 'next week', or 'after the war' – common everyday words and phrases, impossible to keep out of an ordinary conversation – in fact almost everything seemed to have some connection. A pretty picture or view would make him wonder how much longer he'd got to appreciate beauty; a car, even the sound of a car, would make him wonder if he'd ever again be able to go on those weekend jaunts to the coast. A house, a lawnmower, a potting shed, a clothes-line, a child, a pram, a toy, a satchel, a school-bell – all those things, and many more, would make him wonder if he'd ever be able to marry, and have a home and children.

If he had to give that thought a name he'd call it 'The Wonder Thought'. Good name, 'The Wonder Thought' – wondering and wondering.

Getting quite dark now – what time was it? Twenty past eleven. Tomlinson saw him glance at the clock and leant across to get a better look for himself, checking it against his own watch, nodding as he sat back, just to show that he too was aware they were nearing the enemy coast. Had it been easier to speak, Mason would have made some remark like 'Won't be long now', but swathed in helmet and oxygen mask, and having to fiddle with the microphone switch, unnecessary talking was such an effort. What with that and the drone of the engines making it necessary, sometimes, to repeat everything several times. Anything but a bold statement, or a definite question or answer, sounded so silly over the phones, because it wasn't made in a natural voice. Silly, like speaking to somebody else's dog, or dancing without a partner.

Mason was glad there was nobody in the crew who did any unnecessary talking. Not like some chaps he'd flown with, always nattering into the intercom. Apart from being irritating, it could cause a lot of trouble, like the time Clynes made one of his idiotic, useless remarks.

What it had sounded like was 'German fighter on the right'. The fact that the rest of the crew all thought Clynes had said that showed it wasn't just a case of nerves. Of course, they were half expecting to hear something of the sort – naturally, flying over Germany in bright moonlight, with no sign of flak. Only a fool like Clynes would think of making a fatuous, unimportant statement at a time like that, but nobody thought of that at the time.

It made a good story in the mess, though, and it was Clynes himself who really made it good. Good storyteller, old Clynes. He got a hell of a laugh telling it round the bar the next night, describing, and acting at same time with arms outstretched, how suddenly the aircraft began to dance all over the sky; then he was the tail gunner, hunched up, yelling, 'Swing her round – I can't see the bastard', while he, Clynes, searched the sky harder than anybody else. It sounded damn funny, over beer, the way he described it, playing both parts.

'Do you think it saw us, Clynes?'

'No idea, I didn't see it. The first I knew …'

'What do you mean, you didn't see it? You're the only one who did.'

'I didn't.'

'What?'

'I didn't see a bloody thing.'

'But it was you who reported it.'

'Me?'

'Then who the hell did?'

Nobody, but the other three all spoke at once and said they'd heard Clynes say he'd seen it.

'Shut up, everybody. Look, Clynes, you definitely said something just before the panic started. What were you saying?'

'I was just telling you about losing my Ronson lighter last night when … "lighter" and "fighter" – oh, Christ (ha ha), I say, chaps, terribly sorry (ha ha ha).'

Then, according to him, everybody spoke at once again, or shouted rather, and as Clynes said, finishing off the story, 'the bleedin' lengwidge was somefink 'orrible'.

Yes, Clynes could put over a thing like that very well. He could be very good company. Quite irresponsible, of course, and a bit overpowering, but good fun in small doses, or at a party. The mess was much quieter without him, and it seemed to have lost some of its character.

It was Clynes who had got everybody into the habit of making sure the telephone earpiece wasn't covered with ink, and the door-handles weren't smeared with treacle. Damned annoying when you got caught, but you missed not having to look out for those things. Sometimes the old habit came back and you almost expected to see Clynes' impish baby face peering at you from behind the blackout curtain.

There was quite an air of gloom in the mess the night after Clynes was listed missing, and that was most unusual, although nobody spoke about it, except to tell anybody who didn't already know that an aircraft was seen to be getting an awful pasting the night before, and was last seen going down with smoke pouring from one engine. It must have been Clynes – and Dwyer, Mills and Coleman.

Bill Bailey seemed to be the only one unaffected by Clynes' absence. Bill couldn't stand Clynes' practical jokes and his irrepressible heartiness. War was serious business with old Bill. He didn't expect to get through his ops, but the longer he kept going the more bombs he could drop on Hitler's Germany. While Clynes was amusing a crowd round the bar with stories, songs or ballet impersonations, Bill would usually be found in a corner somewhere swotting up navigation or getting genned up on a new flying-aid device. Two completely opposite types. As a citizen, Bill would definitely be the more valuable, but, as Mason often told Bill, the world had to have the Clyneses too; otherwise it would be a drab, serious place to live in.

'If you do live, of course', Bill would mutter. 'He probably won't.'

And Bill was right. The world was one Clynes short now. But any day it might be one Bill Bailey short, to balance things up. And again, any day, tomorrow perhaps, the world might be one Leslie Mason short.

What category, Mason wondered, could he put himself in? Not the Baileys or the Clyneses. No definite category, really, because one day he felt like a Bailey and the next like a Clynes. So it wouldn't matter very much if the world did lose a Leslie Mason. There were lots and lots of Leslie Masons, looking to the Baileys and the Clyneses for a lead, using them as yardsticks by which to measure themselves, admiring and attempting to adopt the best points of each. No, it didn't matter when the Leslie Masons went – only a few people would suffer, for purely sentimental reasons. Perhaps the person it mattered to most was himself, because he just didn't want to die. It gave him rather a lonely feeling to think that it didn't matter if the Germans shot him down tonight. His folks would be upset, of course, and his sister, but it wouldn't really matter to them – not materially.

Perhaps being married would have made a difference:

somebody to whom it would really matter. But that was a very selfish view, wanting it to matter to somebody if he got killed. Mason had seen the effect it had on some wives – at least one wife, Tony Devereaux's. It was lucky she had no children to worry about – they'd only been married two months – but it would have been very silly to have told her that.

What a day off that had been. It had begun by waking up to a cold, thin rain washing away the last of the snow which had been hanging around for weeks.

Walking across to the mess for breakfast just before nine – they had taken off at four the previous day and were back by midnight – he had met the C.O.

'Oh, Mason', the C.O. said as they met in the roadway that led from the Ops Room, 'I'm glad I've seen you.'

'Good morning, sir.'

'I was hoping you would do something for me.' The C.O. smiled to show he would consider it a favour.

'I should think so, sir.'

'Well, it's about Devereaux, or his wife, rather – you knew we lost an aircraft last night?'

'I knew one hadn't got back here. It's missing, is it?'

'I'm afraid so.' The C.O. looked as though he had been up all night. He went on: 'I hear you know his wife.'

Didn't quite like the sound of that. 'Well, I've been about with them several times, and round to their digs.'

'That's what I understood. Well, the point is this – the Padre is on leave, my wife is laid up, and I'll be busy all the morning.' The C.O. was quite serious now. 'And

I was wondering if you wouldn't mind going to see her for me. I'll go along as soon as I can', he said, and added: 'In any case I'd like her to hear it first from somebody she knows.'

It was a task Mason could well do without. It wasn't the sort of thing anybody would relish doing, but the C.O. was perfectly genuine and wasn't trying to slide out of doing it. He was waiting for a reply.

'All right, sir. I'll go now.'

'Good man. Go down to the Transport Section and get them to run you there.' The C.O. was grateful. 'And thanks awfully.'

It was still raining as the transport turned the corner of the road in which the Devereauxs had rooms, and a few houses away Mason told the driver to stop, feeling that there would be something rather impersonal in arriving at the house in an official service car.

As he turned into the gate a curtain in a downstairs room was pushed back further, and Betty Devereaux's face appeared, strained, with staring eyes. In those eyes there was fear, plain fear, not sadness or sorrow, as he had vaguely expected, because she must have known by now that something terrible had happened, and guessed what it was. She knew why he had come, and he knew she knew. It was pointless to smile or wave or anything. Not only pointless; it would be unkind because it might raise her hopes.

The door was opened before he got there and she stood aside to let him enter. She closed the door gently and turned to face him. What little hope she had been nursing was fast diminishing.

'It's Tony', she said.

'Yes, the C.O. asked me to tell you.'

A hand went to her mouth, a thumbnail clicking against her teeth. She wasn't looking at him as she said, without hope, 'There's no chance?'

How he wished, for her sake, he could say there was. Instead: 'I'm only going on what the C.O. told me, you see, Betty. There was no word from the aircraft from the time it left, and …'

'But they might have baled out. Mightn't they?' Oh God, she was clinging to a hope, pleading with him to say there was a chance, no matter how slight.

'No, Betty. The aircraft was seen – at least, an aircraft was seen and all the others came … it couldn't have been any of the others.'

She looked frightened, dazed, lost. 'But … but, in the dark, couldn't somebody have baled out and not been noticed?' Amazing how selfish people get on certain occasions. 'Somebody', she said. One person – Tony.

'Sorry, Betty, the crew who reported it are all sure.'

Mason hoped he wouldn't have to tell her why the crew were so sure – that they saw the aircraft blow up and fall in small burning pieces.

But it seemed that her last dwindling hope, kept alive somehow, had now faded and died. The first appearance of tears began to show in her eyes and she dropped her head. Soon she was sobbing quietly.

A door behind her was open, and he tried to lead her into the room, but she stopped him. 'No', she said, 'no, I must go out. Will you wait for me?'

She didn't want to go anywhere in particular. They walked around the town in the rain, and all the while she kept asking the same questions, often answering them herself. She was fighting desperately to bring that little hope back to life again, but reality was winning, because eventually, very slowly, her conversation was becoming normal – more realistic.

Then suddenly: 'I know what I'm going to do', she said, her voice by contrast quite bright. 'I'll go home. My parents live in Bedford. I'll go tonight.'

He walked back to the house with her, and leaving her there, conscious that he would probably never see her again, thus breaking another link, made his way back to camp.

X

Tomlinson interrupted him by tapping him on the knee. This was it – Tomlinson was going to tell him they were due over the Dutch coast, and Mason looked at him to make sure. Tomlinson nodded towards the clock and pointed ahead.

Nothing to be seen yet, apart from the sea. Couldn't see much of that either. It was pretty dark down there now; they wouldn't see the coast until they were over it. Mason switched on his mike.

'Just about to cross the coast, Dent.'

'OK. I'm not nervous.' Dent seemed almost glad something might be going to happen at last.

'Better get the bomb gear ready, Harper.'

'Righto. What height?'

'Eight thousand, so far.'

'Eight thousand, right.'

Harper too seemed quite pleased to do something. Voice rather high-pitched. A trace of breathlessness, though.

Tomlinson was peering out of the window, occasionally glancing back to the map on his knee. He would be furious if his dead-reckoning was more than a minute or two out.

Better see if Holt was all right.

'You alright, Holt?'

'Yes, everything seems to be working. Will you want me to chuck any flares out tonight?'

'Shouldn't think so. I'm hoping the others have started a fire or two.'

Still no sign of the coastline. Tomlinson was getting a trifle anxious. Suddenly he leant a little more forward, cupping his hands round his eyes. A second or two later he sat back, with a triumphant thumbs-up.

There it was, all right. A little line of white, with a denser sort of blackness beyond.

It was peculiar how different it looked from a friendly coastline. It wasn't different, of course. All coastline looked the same, but crossing into enemy territory Mason always felt he could see something sinister in that little line of white and the vague sort of blackness beyond it. That was one thing the Germans couldn't camouflage, that narrow fringe of surf. He could never understand why that tiny white line always showed up so plainly – well, not exactly plainly, but it was there. It was understandable in rough weather, when the waves crashed and tumbled in foam onto the beach; but in calm weather, when looking at it from the ground, it didn't look as though there was any surf to speak of. And yet, from the air, that line could always be seen. It was calm down there now – must be – but there was the surf-line.

He was getting that funny sort of feeling he always

got when crossing the enemy coast: that tight feeling in his limbs, almost like stiffness.

Oh Christ, that fluttery feeling was coming on again. His arms, even on the arm-rests, were beginning to shake. And his legs. Made him want to sit up straight, press his feet against the rudder-bar, and grip the control column hard. His whole chest seemed to be pumping, not just his heart. Not only was he now shivering all over, but now and again an extra quiver jerked through his body. Tomlinson tapped him again and he turned his head sharply round to him, realising too late that the movement might have given him away. Mustn't let him think he was scared. Oh God, what was he scared of? It didn't seem like ordinary fear – he was scared of being scared. Tomlinson didn't seem to have noticed anything. Gave no sign, anyway – he was holding out the pad with the new course written down. Mustn't take it, though; his hand would give him away. Just look at it and nod. 144 degrees. He turned back and altered the compass, flexing his arm muscles to steady his hand, not looking at Tomlinson again. Out of the corner of his eye he could see that Tomlinson was sitting back in his usual half-slouching position and appeared to have noticed nothing. That was a great relief.

Relief; he felt relieved. Something inside him told him that the feeling was going, although outwardly he felt the same. Trying not to let Tomlinson suspect anything had done the trick. It hadn't gone yet, but he knew now that it would go, and began to feel better. He never minded it when it was going. It took a minute or two, during which time his hands and legs still wanted to shake, and if he spoke his voice would sound unnatural; but knowing it was going, getting less and less every second, was something to look forward to, and consequently increased the speed of its going.

He could look at it squarely now: think about it, wonder about it, without fear of it starting up again. That was the whole thing – being frightened of it. He knew that, but could do nothing about it when it started. There was always plenty of warning, too, when he looked back, but he could never recognise the warnings in time. Once it had started there was no use in saying to himself, 'Ah, here it comes – I'm not frightened of it', because it did make him frightened, and it surged on relentlessly, stiffening his limbs, flooding his chest, trying to choke him. At this moment he wasn't frightened of it, but he knew if anything occurred to start it off again, at some later date when he had forgotten all about it, he would be quite helpless. It was like being caught in quicksands and not knowing they were quicksands until you started to struggle, and then of course the more you struggled the deeper you sank, the more frightened you became, and so the more you struggled.

He couldn't speak to anybody about it, because it would be so difficult to describe and explain. It would sound so damn silly in the security and comfort of a bar or dining room, and it might so happen that the persons he mentioned it to would be people who had never known real fear. In which case they might laugh, or hurriedly change the subject, only to re-open it when he'd gone, and snigger, or shake their heads sadly. He could have told Roger, and Ken. It was the sort of thing he would have automatically told Roger in the course of conversation. With Ken he would have told it laughingly, at first, thus making sure Ken knew what he was talking about. Roger would have known right away.

That, of course, was the difference between the two friendships. Ken he had met in wartime, only in wartime, when everybody had started living an excited, tense, unreal existence. Mason wondered if they would have been such good friends in peacetime. When he came to think of it, they only ever talked seriously on war subjects, or things that came within the framework of war. In that respect, they had a great deal in common. They had the same outlook regarding one's duty, or conscience, or whatever it was called. The same fears, the same type of wartime humour. During training they were baffled by the same problems, jibbed at the same seemingly petty restrictions, which, they always agreed, appeared to have no connection with learning to fly a bomber over Germany.

Somebody switched a mike on.

'Pretty quiet tonight, aren't they? No guns, no lights, no fighters', Dent said.

'Wait till we pick up the Rhine', Mason told him. 'They'll know more or less where we're going then.'

He could just imagine what was going on down there.

153

Men huddled over maps and charts in blackout huts and commandeered farmhouses. Searchlight crews and listening posts following their line of flight. Gun-crews waiting for the order to fire, wondering why their officers were being so stupid.

Where was he when Dent interrupted him? Ah, yes – Roger and Ken. There was no doubt his friendship with Roger had had far deeper roots. It had passed all the tests, from boyhood to manhood, from peacetime to wartime. It had even passed the test of Roger's marriage, short though that test was. Roger's last letter proved that. 'Am getting some leave next month', the letter finished, 'and will, of course, be popping over. Don't forget, Von will be with me this time so will you look out for somewhere for us to stay?'

He felt at the time that Roger had been determined to 'pop over' just to show that his marriage had made no difference to their friendship, but he wasn't able to carry it out, because he never did get that leave.

Mason still had that letter. Many times, clearing out a case or drawer, he had come across it and decided to throw it out with the rest, but somehow it always found its way back.

For some reason, thinking of the letter set him thinking about the end of the war. But it was difficult to visualise the end of the war and not being able to say 'I'll nip down to Roger's this weekend'.

My God, visualising the end of the war. Eight thousand feet over Germany, hundreds of miles to go yet before getting back. More the following night, then more, and more, and still more, going on for years. The end of the war – Christ Almighty – like chasing the sun over the horizon. Those people down there were trying to end his war tonight, and if they weren't successful, or the elements didn't help them, they'd go on trying, night after night.

Dent was right about it being quiet down there tonight. There was a flak belt around here somewhere, Mason knew. Perhaps it had something to do with the fact that they were a long way behind the others. As far as the Germans were concerned it was a single aircraft and they would probably want to find out what it was up to. It could be on reconnaissance, or perhaps an aircraft trying out a new device. Perhaps somebody might decide to let it carry out its mission and then try to bring it down, and so get more information. In which case they would more than likely let it get as far inland as it wanted to go, so it would have less chance of getting back.

Whatever the reason for the quietness, it suited him. He had often heard chaps say they were glad when the flak opened up, because it was a relief from the tension and suspense. But he could never see that. Waiting for something to happen was rather nerve-wracking, but he preferred the keyed-up sort of feeling to the sheer danger of the flak. Being keyed-up was unpleasant, but it didn't blow the aircraft to bits. Wouldn't get much sympathy if you walked into the mess and said, 'Christ, I was keyed-up last night – not a shot fired at us'.

Must be getting near the Rhine now. He switched on the mike.

'How far to the Rhine, Tommy?'

Tomlinson came to and switched his mike on.

'Two minutes – not more than three.'

Didn't realise they were so close. 'Harper, keep your eyes peeled and sing out. We'll turn as soon as we see it.'

'Righto. Who's doing the bombing – Tommy or me?'

'Tommy will do it; you can swap places when nearer.' And because the implication might have offended Harper, Mason added: 'You'd better be up here.'

'Oke.'

'What?'

'I said "Oke" – OK.'

Bloody silly expression to use. Especially over the intercom. Why the hell couldn't people speak clear English? Like those blokes who couldn't talk without using expressions like 'bang on' and 'whacko' and 'prang'. He couldn't stand the word 'kite', either. Why not say 'aircraft' or 'aeroplane'?

There was only one of those expressions Mason liked: 'ring twitter'. Rather good, really; and anyway, it was a definite expression and was used as a substitute for something else. Very true too, apparently. He wondered what it was called before somebody thought of 'ring twitter', because the complaint, if you could call it that, was as old as fear.

Poor old Wood, he had ring twitter that night over Berlin. And then kept it quiet on the way back. After they'd landed, standing in the dark waiting for the tender to arrive, Wood had stood a little away from the rest of them, and judging by his limited conversation was trying to find a reason for not going with them to the Ops Room for interrogation.

Sensing something was wrong, Mason had walked over to Wood, and even in the dark could see that he was embarrassed and unhappy. Out of earshot he said to him, 'What's wrong, cock?'

'Wrong? Oh, nothing really, I …' Then, giving way, Wood said confidingly, 'Oh Christ. I've had a touch of the screamers.' He seemed almost ready to burst into tears with misery and shame.

It was no good telling him it was nothing to be ashamed of, because Wood was the sort of fellow who felt those things acutely. So Mason said to him, 'Well, look – that's all right. I'll tell the Ops Room you're groggy, and have gone straight to bed. Do you feel like coming back in the tender with us?'

'Better not – in that confined space. They'll notice.' Poor devil, he'd been so ashamed and miserable and was pathetically glad to have someone to confide in who wasn't laughing at him.

'Find something to do in the aircraft and I'll send the transport back for you', he told Wood. 'I'll fix the others.' Wood only said, 'Thanks', but he meant far more than that.

Harper's voice came through the phones, a little excited: 'There it is, straight ahead.'

'Right, we'll go down the left bank as far as the bend, then cut straight across and follow the right bank. We won't turn in until we're opposite the target. OK, Tommy?'

'I get you.'

'Perhaps you'd better change places now. Keep your eyes on the river; mustn't miss the bend.'

Unclipping his intercom socket, Tomlinson slid into the well and waited there for Harper to come out of the front turret.

Might as well make the first turn now. Mason wanted to keep as far from the river as possible but still keep it in sight. No need for compass bearings now. Visibility was excellent and all they had to do was follow the river until they found the target. According to the Intelligence Officer at the briefing that shouldn't be difficult. 'Can't miss it', he'd announced, although he had never done a trip. 'After this sharp right-hand bend, just keep your eye on the left bank, and then just where the canal comes in here, you'll see the refinery, standing out like a signpost.' Bloody fool. Talking as though they were on a navigation exercise at home. 'Just follow the left bank and you'll come to it', he repeated as they began to file out. Silly bugger.

'I suppose he thinks we're going to stooge along dead over the river, and make quite sure the Germans guess where we're going.' With a start Mason realised he was talking to himself. Muttering anyway, which was probably worse. The word sounded worse, somehow. It suggested the vocal equivalent of drooling. Good thing the mike wasn't on.

Harper had taken his place in Tomlinson's seat. What a difference there was between the two. Harper was leaning forward with his elbows on his knees, his eyes darting about but not really looking at anything. Better give him something to do.

'Keep your eyes on the river, Harper, will you? I don't see it from this side. You know the bend we're looking for? Have you seen it before?'

'No, I've done a Cologne trip but we didn't come this way. I think I'll recognise it, though.'

Tomlinson might be a little piqued at having somebody detailed to cross-check him.

'Just a double-check, Tommy.'

'Good idea. We should be getting some fireworks any moment now, and pin-pointing won't be so easy then.'

God, yes. Where was the flak? Most uncanny. There probably weren't fighters around either, or there'd be searchlights. Dent, surely, would have mentioned it if he'd seen any lights.

'Seen anything yet, Dent?'

'Not a thing. They know we're here, I suppose?'

'Should do. I rang the bell.' That seemed to amuse Dent.

Holt broke in. 'It's rather odd, when you remember that five other aircraft came this way about half an hour ago. We can hardly have surprised them.'

'Well, they probably don't realise we should have been with them', Mason answered.

Tomlinson had his own ideas. 'We'll find out soon enough', he said. 'Probably some fiendish Jerry trick. Perhaps this isn't the Rhine at all – just a dummy – and we'll finish up in the middle of the Alps, or somewhere.'

Whatever the reason for the inactivity, let it carry on like that. Let them plot and scheme down below, or argue – it just meant there was that much less flak to face.

The only thing that really worried Mason about the lack of flak was the possibility that the Germans were trying out something new, something revolutionary. Like the fighter gadget that Intelligence had warned them about. Nobody had encountered it yet; nobody who had got back, anyway. Pretty deadly, if there was anything in it, because it gave you no chance at all.

Intelligence didn't even know if there was any truth in it, so they said. All they would say was that it was some sort of 'magic eye' fitted to an aircraft, which could pick out an object in the dark, possessing far greater strength than any human eye. That's all they knew, they said. Fat lot of good that was. No point in saying anything about it at all if they couldn't suggest a way to counteract it, or avoid it. All very well to say, 'Look out for a small red glow. If you are lucky you might just see it.'

Christ, the sky was full of them if you looked hard enough.

Better remind Dent, all the same.

'Dent, you haven't forgotten about the "magic eye", have you? You know, the flying glow-worm, or whatever it is we're supposed to look out for.'

'No, I haven't forgotten. Haven't seen anything, though.' Dent seemed quite disappointed.

'Don't wait to make sure. If you do think you've seen anything, yell out right away.'

'You bet.'

He had every confidence in Dent. Not a frightfully bright chap, perhaps, but never let go of a thing once he'd got it. Keen too, in a nice cheerful sort of way. Mason wondered how old Dent was. Difficult to say – anything between nineteen and 24. His manner and speech were young, but his looks were older.

It was the other way round with Tomlinson; he acted older than he looked, and was. But Mason knew Tommy was 24 – that made a difference, knowing his age.

Holt would be about 21 and Harper a little older, say 22 or 23.

So, at 26 Mason was the oldest in the crew. But he was used to that now.

He could remember his surprise on first discovering how young most of the aircrew were. There were only three that he knew of who were his age, apart from instructors, station commanders, and so on: Bill Bailey, Barry and Trewsom. Ken was a year younger.

What was the name of that very young fellow? Killed on ops training. Pagram. Just eighteen. He didn't look old enough to wear long trousers, let alone be a tail gunner, liable to be called upon to save the lives of four other men. Tiny little chap with a childish face.

There were plenty of nineteen year-olds. That little fool Simons – always jumping out from behind doors onto people; dipping rolled-up bits of paper in ink and flicking them across the room on the end of a ruler. Things one did at school. A pilot too. What must some of the old regulars think of this new Air Force?

Harper tapped Mason's arm and pointed ahead. That must be the bend in the river.

'The bend? What do you think, Tommy?'

'I think so. Better carry on for a bit, to make sure.'

Yes, they'd better carry on for a bit, but Mason wished he could speed up the aircraft. Wanted to get there quickly now. He felt a twinge of impatience, almost resentment at Tomlinson's suggestion. Not that he would dream of ignoring the suggestion, but he had hoped it was time to turn, and was already mentally embarking on the last lap to the target. It would have been stupid to turn before making sure, but that wasn't the point – he wished they were at the bend, instead of near it. He was getting keyed-up, that's what it was, not impatience.

Tomlinson spoke, clipping his first word through being too hasty.

'…s'it all right. You'll see it when you turn.'

Tommy's voice sounded different: more businesslike, urgent, and – yes, impatient. It sounded as though he, too, had been a trifle irked by the necessity for making sure.

The stars began to glide round as Mason put the

aircraft into a right-hand turn. He liked watching that, normally – just as though the aircraft was stationary and the sky revolving.

The river came into view. It was like a silver ribbon, with a silky sheen on it, twisting and curling away into the darkness. He hadn't realised it but there was a moon now, full and bright, the pattern standing out like a globe map. It was the moon that gave the river that lovely cold, sad colour: silver with the slightest tinge of blue.

They wouldn't be able to identify the target this far from the river, but he didn't want to go any closer until it was necessary. No doubt Tomlinson would have worked out the flying time.

'How long before we're there, Tommy?'

'If you turn twenty minutes from now we should be somewhere near it. I'm just swotting up the target area now, and if we go in on the bombing course, I think I could pick out the target on the first run.'

'That'll be fine – we might be able to do it in two runs.'

'I think we'll have to. We'll be the only ones over the area, remember. What is your record number of runs?' Tommy was in a chatty mood now.

'Six – on Kiel. Another one would have finished me.'

'I did five one night, with Trewsom, on the *Scharnhorst* in Brest. They put up some stuff that night – on the last run we seemed to fly into a solid wall of flak.'

'I know – I've done a *Scharnhorst* trip.'

Mason purposely made his tone rather abrupt

because he wanted to stop Tomlinson. No point in talking about those things just before they were due to do it again. Going home was the time for that. He was feeling reasonably calm, and wanted to stay that way.

That must be the worst feeling in the world: flying straight and level into an inferno of bursting shells, all around, above and below, conscious that the aircraft was more of a menace than a protection. There seemed to be some hidden force that made you stick there, all the time wanting – trying to find some justification – to abandon the whole thing and get the hell out of it. Listening to that voice: 'Left ... left ... right a little. Hold her there.' Such long pauses between each word, only luck or chance stopping one of those shells from bursting in the aircraft, or near enough to wreck it. Hoping, praying that the voice wouldn't say, 'Round again'. And when it did, the horrible feeling that panic might make it impossible to face another run-up. Had to, though. It was the peak of every trip. That's what the machine had been made for, the trip planned for, the whole Air Force established for.

The sweet relief of hearing 'Bombs gone' sometimes made it all seem worthwhile. It was exciting to stick the nose down and get the maximum speed out of the machine. The bursting flak appeared far less dangerous, because the half-way mark had been passed. Being able, for the first time that trip, to think of 'home' – the friendly greetings of the ground crew, the first cigarette in the tender, another one in the crew-room while changing; the easy atmosphere at interrogation, a meal always ready.

After that the luxury of a bed, the pleasant tiredness of the body, the relief in being able to close smarting eyes, and the strange silence after the drone of the engines. Wondering dreamily what to do with a free day ahead. 'Bombs gone' – if there was any pure excitement in a trip, that was the moment. Like getting on the top of a hill and being able to see the objective, the descent easier.

Mason tried to think of it now, but it didn't work. It wasn't the first time he had tried to think of the 'going home' lap before the half-way mark had been passed, and it had never worked. Many a time, like tonight, he had said to himself, 'Well, just pretend you're on the way home', but always some other voice kept pushing its way in, saying, 'Don't be ridiculous – there's all that flak to face yet'.

The second voice might be some unconscious sense which prevented him from becoming too optimistic and relaxed, so that if the half-way mark wasn't reached the shock wouldn't be so great. It would be very pleasant to be able to imagine himself on the way home, but perhaps he should be thankful to that inner sense, because should anything occur he would be more prepared for it, and there would be the minimum time-lag between the event happening and the realisation that it had happened.

He found that thought quite a consolation. Now that was odd: finding consolation in a positive way from a negative approach. On second thoughts, it wasn't odd, it was natural. One was just make-believe and the other was solid fact. To gain consolation from an answer arrived at by the weighing up of facts was far better than from a whole string of fanciful day-dreams.

Somebody was coming through on the phone. Tomlinson wanting to know if the bombing height was still to be eight thousand feet.

It was a hard thing to decide now they were so near the target. There was going to be a lot of flak, and eight thousand was pretty low. The Germans were getting damned accurate, not like in the old days when you waited until the cluster of bursts crept up on you before turning away. On the other hand it was a fine night for fighters.

But still, there'd been no fighters so far, and between the coast and the target was where they were usually encountered, not often over the target area.

Tommy again: 'What do you think?'

'Sorry, Tommy, I was trying to think. Perhaps we'd better go to nine thousand. Yes, let's make it nine.'

'I think that's wiser. OK then, nine thousand.'

'Incidentally', Tommy went on, 'it seems fairly certain none of the others are hanging around. We would see the flak from here.'

''Fraid so. Never mind, perhaps the Jerries have used up all their ammo on them.'

'I'll remind you of that remark tomorrow.'

Tommy said that so easily and naturally. It didn't seem to have occurred to him that they might not be seeing each other tomorrow.

Tommy was like that in the mess too, talking about

the last op as though it had been nothing more than a rather exciting job of work, at times becoming quite indignant because the Germans had given him such a pasting. Plenty of fellows affected the same attitude, but in nearly every case it was easy to tell that it was, after all, affectation, or lack of imagination. Tommy was quite natural. He was quietly, supremely confident, never speculating on his chances of getting through – just acting as though he expected to.

Even when things were going badly, Tommy was just the same: even on the Bremen trip, when things couldn't have been worse; even when they arrived over Bremen and found solid ten-tenths cloud stretching as far as the eye could see, with a bright moon above reflecting off the clouds making the air in which they were flying as bright as summer twilight, and over on their right they saw a fighter swoop down on another bomber, sending it spiralling through the clouds – even then Tomlinson had the breath to say: 'There's nothing I would like better than to drag the Met Officer out of bed when we get home and bring him straight back here. Three-tenths cloud be buggered.'

What a waste of men's lives and aircraft it was that night.

'There's bad weather on its way across', the Met Officer had said, 'but there won't be much cloud when you get there, and you'll race it back. It will be clear over England until about four o'clock.'

But they'd met the cloud half-way across the North

Sea, at above five thousand feet, well below them, and it got steadily thicker all the way. When they got to the target area they could plainly see other bombers cruising around looking for an opening.

The Germans hadn't bothered about flak that night – they shone the lights onto the bottom of the cloud, causing more brightness above, and sent up the fighters. For the fighters the bombers underneath them made perfect targets against the white, illuminated clouds.

After flying around for five or six minutes it had been obvious there was no break in the cloud anywhere and it was too dangerous to hang about.

'This is no good. We're going back', Mason had told the crew, and as he said it, Tomlinson shouted, 'Look at that!', pointing to the bomber on their right being shot down. The tracers from the fighter raked the length of the bomber, there was a puff of smoke which quickly developed into an increasingly thick trail, one wing dropped and she went over onto her back into the clouds.

Dent yelled through the phones: 'Look out … more fighters … Christ, there are dozens of 'em!'

The light, though unpleasantly bright, had been deceptive. Perhaps Dent …

'Three of them – above – they're diving!'

Mason had taken Dent's word for it and stuck the nose down. The only thing to do was to get into those clouds.

Down lower, and in front another bomber was trying to do the same thing, a fighter chasing it, diving almost vertical.

A violent clatter came through the intercom as Tommy in the front turret opened up on the fighter with his single gun. The fighter, surprised, veered off and climbed away.

'They're almost on us!' Dent yelled from behind.

The intercom rattled and chattered again as Dent's four guns opened fire. One burst ... silence. Was Dent all right? Another burst ... thank God ... and another.

'Got 'im! Got 'im! Look on the port side.'

Over on the left one of the fighters was plunging into the clouds on fire.

'Where are the other two, Dent?'

'They over-shot and are going round for another go. Above us – port side. See them?'

Mason had looked over his shoulder and seen them, up high, finishing a circle to begin their next dive. The cloud-top was getting nearer, but ...

Tommy came in: 'The one I had a go at is going to come in from the side, I think, same side. Yes, here he comes.'

Mason looked but couldn't see the other one – all the same, he turned the aircraft to get Dent in line. Dent should be able to cover all three now. Everything in the aircraft was shuddering and the cloud was getting nearer. Nearer.

As the first wisp of cloud dispersed on the wind-screen, several lines of tracers streaked over their heads, and simultaneously Dent's guns opened up. They were still firing as the aircraft surged deep into the cloud, and now, for the moment, they were safe. But for how long? There was the flak to worry about now. And only five thousand feet.

Mason had reset the compass and turned the aircraft in the rough direction for home.

Tommy hadn't waited to be told to come out of the front turret – he knew he'd be needed in the cabin now. They weren't carrying a second pilot that night so Tommy had to do it all, taking it in his stride. After a few minutes he handed the new course over – nobody spoke about the fighters they had just shaken off because they all knew they weren't in the clear yet.

They had flown along blindly through the cloud for ten minutes in silence. Mason nudged Tomlinson at his side, indicating that he was going to speak to him.

'I think we can chance it now, don't you?'

'I should think so. There's a bit of ice in the wings.'

'That's what I was thinking.'

They had begun to climb and soon the aircraft was nosing her way through the thin layers of the cloud-top, all eyes scanning the sky.

Mason couldn't understand why there wasn't any flak, unless it was because the fighters were all round here too.

Almost as though it was a signal, the flak had started. The first burst was in front and below them, then several more, keeping that much in front of them, but getting higher. A cluster came up in rapid succession on their right, about the same height. It was unpleasantly close but Mason expected more. He swung the aircraft away to the left as Dent called: 'Flak behind – not close, and too high.'

A sudden series of bursts in front, level with them, shook the aircraft, and almost immediately they flew through the smoke, the smell of cordite filling the cabin. They waited for more from the same batch of guns, but nothing happened. If the commander of the gun-post which had fired that last burst had known how near they had been, he would have kept on. Then the other batteries stopped, and everything was quiet.

'Keep a look out, everybody.'

Tomlinson, leaning forward scanning the sky, looked as though he was on a routine flight.

There was no further trouble and they had crossed the North Sea in peace.

Working on a radio fix that Holt had got for him, Tomlinson said: 'We should be over the English coast now.'

They had begun to descend through the cloud, which got thicker and darker the lower they dropped. At three thousand feet they met really dirty weather: heavy, driving rain and a considerable amount of turbulence. At one thousand feet Holt said he had contacted the aerodrome on the R/T and they were overhead, but the ground was blotted out and Control had warned that landing conditions were bad.

Mason had put the aircraft into a shallow left-hand turn, losing height, and gazed down at where the ground should be, but could see nothing. Tomlinson went down into the nose to get a less obstructed view.

Circling at a few hundred feet they occasionally caught glimpses of the airfield lights through the swirling clouds and rain, and Mason couldn't help wondering if there were any other aircraft circling at the same height.

Suddenly he had seen the end of the flare-path, the cloud which had been obscuring it racing along its entire length until the whole runway was visible for one brief moment, and then it was gone; but he memorised the direction before making a wide sweep, and turning in, dropped height.

On the approach, losing height rapidly, the flare-path came into view, but never the whole length at the same time until, crossing the aerodrome boundary, he saw the line of lights stretching out in front of him.

The angle of approach was wrong and had to be corrected quickly, and they were too high. Mason pushed the nose down, saw the ground rushing up, flattened out, and landed her heavily, a little too far along the runway, but they were down. Vigorous application of the brakes did the rest.

Tomlinson emerged from the front turret, pushing his helmet off his head and letting it dangle round his neck on the intercom cords.

'We'll have to get the front turret fixed', he said, running a hand through his hair. 'There's a hole in the Perspex about the size of your fist. Flak.' He stretched, twisting his face.

Another op nearer the end of the tour, waste though it was.

XI

Apart from his efficiency as a navigator, Tomlinson was a very useful bloke to have in the crew, for his calm confidence. If his confidence meant anything, the whole crew would come through safely tonight.

The intercom came on.

'You can't see anything in front, I suppose?' Dent asked. 'No lights or anything?'

Mason almost laughed at Dent's tone. It sounded peevish, like a kid at a circus impatiently awaiting the appearance of the lions.

Tommy broke in before he could answer.

'Sorry, old boy, I'm afraid there's nothing.'

Dent chuckled before continuing, more seriously: 'I don't like this. Too bloody quiet – a bit fishy.'

'As a matter of fact', Tommy replied, rather slowly, 'nor do I. We must have passed over some defended areas. All I can think is that the fighters are about and we've been lucky.'

Tomlinson sounded a little worried as he said that. Well, not worried perhaps – pensive, maybe. Better try and put a stop to that. Wouldn't like to think of Tommy losing some of that confidence.

Mason chipped in quickly, before Dent had a chance

173

to say anything more. 'I still think they are wondering what we're up to.'

'Perhaps you're right.' Tommy sounded dubious, and paused before going on. 'Anyway, we'll soon know. We're about to turn, I should think.'

'Any time now. Can you identify anything?'

'Well, there's a big U-shaped twist over there. I think it's the one we want. The target should be just south of it. Can you see the one I mean?'

Looking over to the left, Mason could just make out the peculiar shape the river took just there.

'I think I can see the one. We'll make for it. Let me know as soon as you identify it. Turning now.'

'OK.'

Tommy was his old self again.

The nose of the aircraft swung round and headed for that deep bend, but at an acute angle. Mason would keep it there until Tommy had picked out the target, then fly parallel with it until they were opposite. Then run in across the river.

If Tommy had made a mistake and this wasn't the pin-point he thought it was, there would be nothing for it but to fly along the river. In that case the Germans would know immediately it was the refinery they were after. Obviously – the others had bombed it already tonight. Probably knew now, anyway: everyone down there at their posts, listening, waiting, giving orders, taking orders. Smart heel-clicking battery commanders hoping it would be another triumph for their particular battery, another star to paint over the door of the mess. Another front page for Goebbels' press: 'British bombers again attempted to penetrate the German defences last night. A hospital and two churches …' etc., etc.

Another ten minutes and it would be over; they would be on the way home. But what a difference ten minutes could make to one's life. Ten minutes. Hardly anything. Just about the time it took to walk from the mess to the crew-room and back. It was the amount of time Mason allowed himself to go from his room to the main gate to catch the half-hourly bus. To go into the town, to The George or The Pheasant, to a dance in the town hall.

They were a long way from The George, The Pheasant and the town hall now. Hundreds of miles, and something else which couldn't be calculated in miles, or time. The next ten minutes would make all the difference to whether they would be catching that bus tomorrow or not. Just ten minutes.

He was startled by Tomlinson suddenly calling: 'That's it all right', and then louder, excited, 'and I can see the refinery – look, just to the right of it – a bloody great black mass, with things sticking up all over the place.'

Mason didn't look – no need to. He'd look when they'd turned. The aircraft swung due south, and now he saw it. Not straight away. It was further from the bend than he thought, but having seen it, there was no mistaking it. It was the target, right enough – huge oil containers, chimneys, buildings, small peeping lights.

He looked hard at it, because there was something else that caught his attention, a small red-yellow glow, rising and falling. It was too striking to be ... it looked like a fire. The others had started a fire.

Before Mason could switch on his mike, Tomlinson yelled: 'There's a fire. Can you see it?'

'Yes, I can. Not a dummy, I suppose?'

'No, can't be, it's slap in the middle of the target – beauty.'

'That's fine. If we don't score a bull, it's nice to know somebody has.'

'We've got something to report when we get back, anyway.' Tommy was tickled pink. His optimism was a tonic.

They were catching up on the dark, irregular-looking mass now, over on the left.

Mason wondered if this turning off the target could possibly have fooled the Germans. Shouldn't think so, but this quietness was uncanny. It was the Ruhr down there, not a vast tract of desert.

Something brushed against him and he looked round. Harper was standing at his side peering over him at the target. Mason wanted to look at his face to see what he looked like now. Moving his head quickly, he took a glance, but didn't learn much because he couldn't see Harper's eyes. What he could see of his face was, perhaps, a little pale, but then his own probably was too.

Harper sat down again, looking down the other side, leaning forward. Seemed all right.

They were level with the target – just about. Mason had to steady his hand as he fumbled the mike switch. It wasn't that fluttery feeling, though: there was nothing in his legs. His jaw felt tight, but it wasn't trying to shiver. He could speak normally.

'OK, Tommy, stand by. Here we go.'

Tommy's voice was perfectly calm as he answered: 'Standing by, mind the women and children.' Tommy left his mike switched on – you didn't have to tell him these things. Better tell the others.

'Keep your mikes on, everybody.'

They were heading for the refinery, keeping the flickering red light dead centre.

'Keep just like that.' Tommy said that to show he was in position and standing by.

They were well over the town; the overflow on the other side of the river. No flak yet – where the hell was it? The aircraft was flying smoothly and level, the engines perfectly synchronised.

'That fire gives a beautiful—' Tommy's words were swamped by a terrific crackling explosion somewhere under the tail, followed immediately by others, all round, the sounds so close together that they overlapped. The sky was full of orange flashes, both sides, above and below. And a white light – everything was dazzling white. Couldn't see beyond the windows, except the flashes. The cordite fumes, thick as fog, were stinging Mason's throat, choking him. The aircraft wanted to climb and go left. He had to push hard to keep on course. Harper was

177

standing, crouching, not looking. Must get out of these lights. The air must be full of shrapnel; it was going some-where. Couldn't hold the aircraft. Push hard … keep on course … target was just ahead. This was fear – plain fear, not panic. Couldn't possibly survive. Must stop soon – couldn't go on for ever.

If they got out of this … With a sickening jolt that jarred his whole body the aircraft shuddered and lurched to the left. The port engine went dead: feather the prop quickly. Oh my God – flames. The engine was on fire. Couldn't be, this couldn't happen. Must be some way out. She was well alight. Hopeless, helpless.

'Drop the bombs, we've been hit.' Didn't mean to shout like that. Tommy was a long time. 'Hurry, Tommy.'

'Bombs gone.'

What now?

'Come back, Tommy, we've had it.'

Harper was fixing his parachute feverishly, fumbling badly. Of course, must bale out. Tell the others. Was there nothing that could be done? Baling out was so final, so deliberately cutting off all hopes of getting back. No, nothing. Have to hurry too.

'Bale out. Bale out.' Dent might have been hit. 'Dent!'

'Right. Going now. Good luck, Leslie.'

Everything had gone quiet suddenly. The flak had stopped. Only the lights. Tommy was standing there, his 'chute on. Harper was in the well, opening the hatch. There was a rush of air as it opened. Bloody fool was going out with his oxygen pipe and phone cable dangling all round him.

'Harper, your …'

Harper went through the hatch – just his fingers showing now. They went suddenly.

Mason felt a pat on his right shoulder. Holt passed, jumped into the well, waved a hand and went out.

There was a sudden brittle, splintering noise – and a violent blow just in from Mason's left shoulder shook his whole body. The side windscreen and window were shattered. Must have been hit. He was numb all down one side, and dizzy. Just under his collar bone. Like being hit with a hammer. No flak – a fighter then. He'd been hit by a bullet. Thought it would have been a hot searing pain. Didn't hurt, not really – just a dreadful ache. God, the aircraft was going to stall – nose wanted to go up. Must push harder. Needed two hands, but his left arm wouldn't move. Tommy was shaking his other shoulder speaking to him, his voice coming from a distance.

'Your 'chute, where's your 'chute?'

Mason knew where it was – where he always put it, under the seat, behind him. Couldn't think where that was now, though. Like being upside down, had to work it out. Shocking being dizzy when you wanted to think. If the air-speed dropped any more the aircraft would stall. He could think of that all right. Expect it was because the indicator was in front of him, but his 'chute was somewhere behind. Somebody was fiddling with his oxygen mask – taking it off. That was better, could breathe easier.

Who was it? Ah, Tommy of course. Tommy was helping him. Now with his parachute harness. Tommy. Tommy was fixing his 'chute for him. Good old Tommy, couldn't have done it with one hand. Tommy was shouting at him. Kept saying: 'You all right? Are you all right?'

Yes, he was all right. Only his arm. He could still walk.

'Yes, yes. Go on, Tommy. I can't hold her.'

Something was trickling down his stomach. Must say something to Tommy. Good bloke, Tommy. Hurry, before he goes. Have to shout, he's in the well.

'Thanks, Tommy.'

Tomlinson was on the floor, his legs through the hatch. He turned, grinned quickly, stuck up two fingers and disappeared.

The aircraft was wallowing. Must get out quickly. Mason grabbed the handle above his head with his right hand, hauling himself up. As the control column was released the nose of the machine began to rise and one wing started to drop. His left leg wouldn't work properly. Pins and needles, it felt like.

As he scrambled into the well, the aircraft began to bank steeply to the left. He was on the floor, with his hand gripping the hatch frame. The aircraft was going out of control, practically on its side now. More like trying to climb through a window. He got his feet against the bulkhead and pushed. Head and shoulders were through – oh Christ, the phone cable. Caught somewhere under his body. Couldn't fiddle now, take the helmet off. No time to undo the chinstrap. Hell, it was too tight. Pull harder; something must go. That was better – hurt his ears, though. The good engine was roaring. No fear of falling into the prop; it was above him. Must miss the other engine – could get a nasty clout.

As he heaved, the aircraft stalled and hung in mid-air, then lurched horribly and he was out. It flashed past him, quite plainly against the sky, great chunk missing off the tail, jagged fabric flapping, and it was gone.

He was falling, and it was quiet and peaceful. There was something else he had to do. Oh yes, the rip-cord. He hadn't forgotten – just thinking. When he pulled, the metal ring came away in his hand. He held it in front of him, staring at it stupidly, wondering what to do. Nothing seemed to be happening.

As he was wondering what should happen when a rip-cord was pulled, and if the ring should come away like that, a flurry of cords and silk swept past his face. There should be a jerk now. That's what people said – a jerk. Caught you between the legs, so they said. Sometimes, apparently, if the silk jerked open too quickly, a spark was generated and caught the whole thing alight. Electricity. Funny thing, that – electricity in silk. The silk came from the silkworm. Thousands of little silkworms all breeding like mad to make lots of parachutes. 'Come on, Alfie. Eat up your supper, or you'll never help to make a parachute.'

Did they have to kill the worms to get the silk, or did they just take the silk from them? He wouldn't like to think of all those silkworms being killed. Little Alfie, for instance.

'He died that you might live.' Now where did that come from? Oh yes. Jesus on the Cross. Why think of that? Nothing to do with silk. Was it true that everybody, no matter how boldly they claimed atheism throughout their life, always turned to religion on the point of death? Was it a sign – something beyond one's control?

This jerk was a long time coming; damn thing should have opened by now. Perhaps it wasn't going to open. Perhaps it should have opened a long time ago if it was going to. Maybe it wasn't even attached to him. Clips not fastened properly. It must be that, because he knew it had opened – it all rushed past his face. Anyway, it was no longer on his chest; the pack had gone. He was going down without a 'chute. When he hit the ground he would be killed.

This made him sad, not worried or frightened. After all those trips – flak, fighters, storms and fog; those two crashes, two forced landings, being shot down, getting out, and now no bloody parachute. Well, somebody was having a dirty great laugh.

He couldn't understand why he had a pain between the legs. It hurt quite a lot, and he couldn't remember it happening. Peculiar sort of pain, more like a pressure.

He put his hand down. There was a sort of strap there – two straps, one in each groin, meeting in the middle. It was his parachute harness, but it was tight, just as though something was pulling on it. Just as though he was hanging on his 'chute. Could easily tell by putting his hand up and feeling the shoulder struts. They were there all right, tight and firm. Perhaps if he looked up ... yes, there it was, an enormous dome of white. Huge. How did all that get into such a small pack? Wonderful invention – saved lives. Funny about that jerk, though, didn't feel a thing.

He thought he was going to be sick – felt very dizzy. Felt like coming round after an operation. That's it: he'd been unconscious. That's why he didn't feel the jerk. The last thing he remembered was pulling the rip-cord. Wonder how long for – perhaps he was near the ground. Couldn't tell, though, it was all so vague. Lots of dark patches about. Those must be trees; but they might be bushes, and he was low down. Couldn't get any perspective.

He wished he could be sick. His left arm was aching badly too, the shoulder straps pulling on it. He'd been very lucky there – one bullet in a part where it didn't really matter. A little lower down and it would have got his heart, or a little to the right, through his chest. Must be bleeding a lot; he could feel all that side was wet, warm and sticky. Right down his leg. That might be a separate one, but he couldn't tell. A leg wound was nothing anyway.

A dark shapeless blur, appearing from nowhere, rushed at him. It seemed to hit him everywhere at the same time, legs, head and stomach, thousands of pinpoints of light, and he couldn't breathe. He was gasping for breath.

Getting better now; he could breathe more easily. His forehead hurt where it had been hit. Couldn't think what it could have been. Aircraft flew into him, perhaps. But that would have killed him.

Maybe it had. Nobody knew what death was like. This might be it. Quite likely was; yes, probably was. Funny, though, it felt no different to being alive. Not in his limbs, but outside him, as it were, it could easily be death, because he couldn't see anything. Just a sort of unreal darkness.

He felt very tired. Might as well go to sleep. Make himself comfortable first; there were one or two things digging into his chest and stomach, and his legs were at an awkward angle. He would move his face round a bit too and make it more comfortable.

When he pressed his hand down to move himself, little things dug into it – like stones, or hard earth. All gritty. Just like the ground. It was just like lying on the ground, face down. Better make sure – could do that by turning over. Should be looking up at the sky then. Not easy, though, turning over. His shoulder hurt when his left arm touched anything. The whole arm and shoulder had gone stiff. If he could get onto his right side he could roll over onto his back. Got it … now take a breath, and push with the left leg. The leg wouldn't move, though. It was too heavy. Like lead – his leg had turned to lead, and he didn't have enough strength to lift it.

Have to wriggle over, then. Wished his head didn't ache so. That's it – he was over – damn that arm. There was the sky, but he'd have to get his left arm in a comfortable position before he could think about it. That seemed better – bent with his hand on his stomach. Not the stomach, the diaphragm.

Lots of stars out now. Couldn't see the moon, must be over the back of his head.

He'd like a cigarette; they were in his parachute jacket. Put them there so they wouldn't be pinched back home. The lady in the post office, bless her. They were still there, although the zip wasn't fastened. Wonder what the girl in green was doing now. She might be thinking of him, as he was thinking of her.

His lighter was in his trousers pocket, in his right pocket, should be. Hope so, because it would be difficult to reach his left pocket. Oh blast, all this parachute guff in the way, straps, buckles and things. Wouldn't bother – he was too tired to smoke anyway.

If he was going to sleep he ought to get the parachute and wrap up in it. Probably be chilly later on. Wasn't exactly hot now. In fact, now he came to think of it, he was pretty cold. Better get that 'chute. Hell of an effort to sit up. Didn't seem to be much strength in his right arm now. That was tiredness, of course. Must have lost a lot of blood too – that made you weak. Sleep, that's what he wanted. Get that 'chute and go to sleep. Couldn't get up; his left leg was useless and his right leg wouldn't support him. Crawl then. Not so easy, though, trying to crawl on one hand and one knee, especially as that arm wouldn't hold his weight. Would have to get along like this, on the elbow. Take the weight on the right knee, and jump the elbow forward – oh Christ, his arm, no, that was no good: back where he started on his face. Couldn't get up at all now. Oh, to hell with the parachute, he'd sleep like this. So tired he could sleep anyhow, anywhere. Wouldn't even try to turn over.

He was on the ground, that's all that mattered. No more ops. Couldn't do any more. He'd done his. Nobody would ask him to do any more. They wouldn't dare, surely? Couldn't stand another one. No, of course they wouldn't. He'd had what was coming to him, and happened to survive. If he'd been killed he couldn't have gone again, so why punish him for being lucky enough to get through? No. No more ops ... never wanted to fly again. Just wanted to sleep. To sleep for as long as he'd been doing ops; he'd catch up then. Sleep was nice at all times, especially nice now, being so tired. Would go back to The George one day. And The Unicorn, and The Barley Mow. Wouldn't be any of the old crowd there, though – Ken, Trewsom, Millet, Barrett ... He'd go back all the same, on his own, to have a quiet drink with them. Not that Cenotaph business – he wanted to remember them living, not to remind himself that they were dead. Just on his own – not even the girl in green. Wood, Clynes ... and Wright, and Dwyer and ... couldn't think of the others. Too tired. Must sleep. Couldn't think any more. Sleep.

XII

The sun had risen in a clear blue sky. The countryside had awakened some time ago, but a few miles over to the right, to where the road apparently was leading, the great industrial town of Düsseldorf was just coming to life.

On that road, but coming from the left, could be heard the tramp, tramp of feet, and male voices singing a marching song.

A party of soldiers swung round the corner. At their head an erect, young-looking lieutenant was setting the pace for the marching and the tempo and volume of the singing.

As they reached the open, gorse-dotted wasteland on their right, the N.C.O., marching behind the officer but ahead of his men, had his eye attracted by a patch of white, partly on the ground, partly enveloping a bush. He stared at it for some seconds, singing mechanically. Having decided that it was something out of the ordinary, he touched the officer's arm and pointed. They both looked, still singing.

The officer stopped singing, and gave orders to stop the men and halt the patrol, and stood back watching until they were standing at ease.

Beckoning to the N.C.O. to follow, he strode off the road towards the patch of white.

As they got nearer the N.C.O. said something and pointed again, to an odd-shaped bundle just beyond what they now identified as a parachute. It was obviously the person who had descended by the parachute. The officer drew his pistol, keeping his eye on the subject.

They could see now that it was a British airman. He didn't stir as they approached and stood over him.

At first they thought he was dead, but when they turned him over, the airman's eyes flickered open for a moment and then closed again, like a person dozing in the sun being momentarily disturbed.

The officer knelt down and gently pulled the airman into a more natural lying position, concluding as he did so that judging by the peaceful expression on the airman's face, his wounds were not so serious as the amount of dried blood suggested.

The officer straightened up, and turning to the N.C.O., ordered him to detail one man to guard the airman and one man to report back to headquarters. The rest would continue the exercise. They both turned and marched towards the road.

The lieutenant looked at his watch. It was seven o'clock.

Acknowledgements

The publisher would like to thank the following for their assistance in preparing this book: Christopher Mann, Anthony Mann and the Leslie Mann Estate, Professor Richard Overy, and the staff of Imperial War Museums, especially Madeleine James and Caitlin Flynn.

Notes

1   This and all subsequent raid details from Martin
    Middlebrook and Chris Everitt, *The Bomber Command
    War Diaries: An operational reference book 1939–1945*
    (Leicester: Midland Publishing, 2000).
2   Martin Gilbert (ed.), *The Churchill War Papers: Volume II:
    Never Surrender, May 1940–December 1940* (London:
    Macmillan, 1994), pp. 17–18, 24–6, 38–43.
3   See Mark Connelly, 'The British People, the Press and the
    Strategic Air Campaign Against Germany, 1939–1945',
    Contemporary British History, 16 (2002), pp. 39–58.
4   Richard Overy, *The Bombing War: Europe 1939–1945*
    (London: Allen Lane, 2013), pp. 547–56.
5   The National Archive (TNA), Kew, London, AIR 20/25, Air
    Intelligence to Directorate of Bomber Operations, 23 May
    1941. On the decision to shift to bombing workers and
    their milieu see Richard Overy, 'The "Weak Link"?: Bomber
    Command and the German Working Class, 1940–1945',
    Labour History Review, 77 (2012), pp. 11–34.
6   TNA, AIR 41/41, RAF Narrative, 'The RAF in the Bombing
    Offensive Against Germany: Vol. III, Area Bombing and
    the Makeshift Force', appendix C.
7   TNA, AIR 22/ 37, Air Ministry War Room Daily Returns,
    Strength of Aircraft July–Sept 1941.
8   TNA, AIR 22/203, War Room Manual of Bomber
    Command Operations 1939–1945, p. 20.

9   TNA, AIR 49/357, E.C. Jewesbury, 'Work and Problems of an RAF Neuropsychiatric Centre', July 1943, pp. 2–4, 10.

10 Ibid., pp. 11–13. See too Edgar Jones, '"LMF": The Use of Psychiatric Stigma in the Royal Air Force during the Second World War', *Journal of Military History*, 70 (2006), pp. 440–44, 452; and Allan D. English, 'A Predisposition to Cowardice? Aviation Psychology and the Genesis of "Lack of Moral Fibre"', *War & Society*, 13 (1995), pp. 15–34.

11 Mark Wells, *Courage and Air Warfare: The Allied Air Crew Experience in the Second World War* (London: Frank Cass, 1995), pp. 204–5.

12 Air Force Historical Records Agency, Maxwell AFB, Alabama, Disc A5385, Eighth Air Force, Growth, Development and Operations, Combat Crew Casualties.

13 Neville Wylie, 'Muted Applause? British Prisoners of War as Observers and Victims of the Allied Bombing Campaign over Germany' in Claudia Baldoli, Andrew Knapp, and Richard Overy (eds), *Bombing, States and Peoples in Western Europe, 1940–1945* (London: Continuum, 2011), pp. 256–78.

14 Leslie Mann to Joan Mann, 22 June 1941. Quotations from Leslie Mann's letters courtesy of Christopher Mann.

15 Leslie Mann to Joan Mann, n.d. but postmarked 30 June 1941.

16 Leslie Mann to Joan Mann, 6 February 1942 from Stalag IX-C.

17 Leslie Mann to Joan Mann, 24 April 1942. A few weeks before he had written 'I'd be happy if I thought I'd see you this year'.

18 Leslie Mann to Joan Mann, 3 August 1943.

HESS, HITLER AND CHURCHILL
The Real Turning Point of the Second World War
– A Secret History

Peter Padfield

'A fascinating work of historical investigation.' *Daily Telegraph*

'Grippingly readable ... the fullest and most convincing exposition of one of the 20th century's strangest stories.' *Sunday Telegraph*

Rudolf Hess's flight to Scotland in May 1941 has been one of the Second World War's greatest mysteries. Now, historian Peter Padfield presents a striking reappraisal of the mission and its significance, demonstrating that the Deputy Führer brought with him a draft peace treaty that had the potential to destroy Churchill's campaign to bring the United States into the war. *Hess, Hitler and Churchill* reveals the hidden story behind the decisive turning point in the Second World War.

ISBN 978–184831–661–4
UK £9.99

JULY 1914
Countdown to War

Sean McMeekin

'A genuinely exciting, almost hour-by-hour account of the terrible month when Europe's diplomats danced their continent over the edge and into the abyss.'   *BBC History Magazine*

'A work of meticulous scholarship ... McMeekin's description of the details of life in the European capitals – small events that influenced great decisions – makes *July 1914* irresistible.'   Roy Hattersley, *The Times*

'Lucid, convincing and full of rich detail, the book is a triumph for the narrative method and a vivid demonstration that chronology is the logic of history.'   *Independent*

'Sean McMeekin is establishing himself as a – or even *the* – leading young historian of modern Europe. Here he turns his gifts to the outbreak of war in July 1914 and has written another masterpiece.' Norman Stone, author of *World War Two: A Short History*

ISBN 978–184831–657–7
UK £9.99

STALIN'S GENERAL
The Life of Georgy Zhukov

Geoffrey Roberts

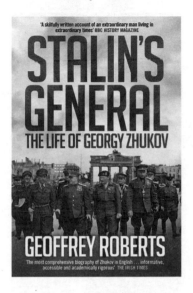

'A skilfully written account of an extraordinary man
living in extraordinary times.' *BBC History Magazine*

Marshal Georgy Zhukov is increasingly seen as the
indispensable military leader of the Second World War,
surpassing Eisenhower, Patton, Montgomery and MacArthur in
his military brilliance and ferocity. He played a decisive role in
the battles of Moscow, Stalingrad and Kursk, was the first of the
Allied generals to enter Berlin, and took the German surrender.
He led the huge victory parade in Red Square, riding a white
horse, dangerously provoking Stalin's envy.

Making use of hundreds of documents from Russian military
archives, as well as unpublished versions of Zhukov's memoirs,
Geoffrey Roberts fashions a remarkably intimate portrait of a
man whose personality was as fascinating as it was contradictory.

ISBN 978-184831-517-4
UK £10.99

ZERO NIGHT
The Untold Story of World War Two's
Most Daring Great Escape

Mark Felton

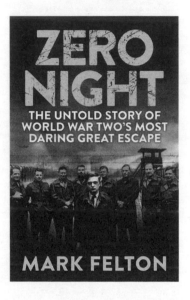

Oflag VI-B, Warburg, Germany: On the night of 30 August
1942 – 'Zero Night' – 40 officers from Britain, Australia,
New Zealand and South Africa staged the most audacious mass
escape of World War Two. It was the first 'Great Escape' – but
instead of tunnelling, the POWs boldly went over the huge
perimeter fences using wooden scaling contraptions.

Telling this remarkable story in full for the first time, historian
Mark Felton brilliantly evokes the suspense of the escape itself
and the adventures of those who eluded the Germans, as well
as the courage of the civilians who risked their lives to help
them in enemy territory. Told with a novelist's eye for drama
and detail, this is a rip-roaring adventure story, all the more
thrilling for being true.

ISBN 978-184831-719-2
UK £16.99

Published October 2014